A CASTLE SEALED

Castle in the Wilde — Prequel Novella

SHARON ROSE

Eternarose Publishing

To Bridgett,
my faithful friend with a discerning eye.

CONTENTS

Fountain Isle
River Thane
Vixicat Lair
Cave Rapids
The Wilde
Tower Woods
Lavaycia
N
E
S
W

CHAPTER 1

In the Border Lands

Those absurd tales of a mysterious castle... Why did they flourish here?

Tristan mulled over the conflicting stories until a sharp gust knifed past his collar. He snugged his wool cloak tighter around his neck. The wind drove swarms of yellow leaves down on his small party of riders. Dark clouds billowed from the horizon, half obscuring the low sun. Rain tonight? Would they be forced to sleep outside in this?

Beside him, Cotrell lifted his head and sampled the air. "Do you smell that?"

"Never as you do," Tristan said.

"Smoke and meat."

"Ah, fine tidings if we may share in it. And what of the tall tales? Do you smell them, as well?"

Cotrell snorted. "Wouldn't surprise me if they tell us that castle floats."

They crested a long rise, and at last, a few buildings came into view. A welcome sight. Tristan raised his arm to signal the rider behind and drew rein. The horses slowed from their running-walk gait to a slow walk, but even still, the few people about town turned to stare as they ambled into the hamlet. Every town smaller than the last. Like forgotten threads, unraveled from Verenlia's frayed border. The inn was small, too, but no matter, for the scent of roasting meat made his mouth water.

An innkeeper with a mop of unruly hair stepped out as they dismounted in the foreyard. "Good eve. How may I serve you?"

"Can you provide dinner, beds, and stable?" Tristan asked.

"Aye. We have roasted boar this eve." The innkeeper pointed up over his shoulder. "We've just the one room, but no other guests tonight." He glanced toward a well-grown lad, who dashed around the corner of the building. "Toby, take charge of the horses." The innkeeper turned back through the doorway as the lad gaped, overwhelmed, by the look of it.

Tristan handed his reins to Cotrell, while James untied the long lead of their extra horse. "Toby," Tristan said, "is it just you in the stable?"

"Aye, sir."

If the lad's worn shirt and short trousers were evidence, he received a pittance from stabling fees paid to the landlord. Tristan fished in his pouch for a coin, and the lad's eyes brightened at the chink. "Then, you'll have plenty to do with rubbing them down and all." Tristan held out a silver coin. "Another in the morn if it's done well."

The lad clutched the coin. "It will be, sir!"

Cotrell uttered a faint huff. "Take those two horses, and I'll follow you." As Toby took the reins from James and led the pair away, Cotrell murmured to Tristan, "I don't see why you hide your title and surname if you're going to flash silver about."

Tristan grinned and strode within, James following. The

common room held a long table with benches down either side. Empty, for now at least. Tristan took a seat, and James settled across from him, glancing around.

Though James looked impassive, Tristan had known him too long to have any doubt what he thought of such places. Accepting, but never comfortable. Especially since he must guard his tongue. 'Twas not easy for a man of nigh fifty to drop formal habits of speech.

The innkeeper brought mugs of ale. "We'll be serving dinner ere long." He hurried away, touched a taper to the kindling fire on the hearth, then began lighting oil lamps.

James took a swallow and set his mug down. Even on this jaunt, he was clean-shaven, with his brown hair combed neatly back.

"Tired?" Tristan asked.

"Not overmuch."

As though he would complain if he were. Tristan exchanged a nod with a couple as they entered. Cotrell followed, with saddle packs slung over his shoulders and a leather bundle that held the map tube and the swords they didn't flaunt. The innkeeper pointed him up the side stairs. After a few thumps overhead, Cotrell returned to join them.

He took a long draw from his ale, then wiped droplets from the chestnut beard curling around his lips. "The stable will do, but we had to evict the cow."

"Does Toby know horses?"

"Well enough. He's anxious to please. Imagine that."

More patrons arrived. Amid the chatter, the innkeeper carried in a board laden with a massive hunk of meat and thumped it down on the far end of the table. A red-cheeked matron in a spattered apron bustled about with bread and bowls of a stewed, orangish vegetable.

Unrecognizable food nudged Tristan's wish for home, but it smelled good and tasted better. Wooden plates with slabs of roast boar were passed down the length of the table, and conversation lulled. There was nothing like hunger to make a simple repast delicious.

Sated bellies gave way to the appetite of curiosity. With practiced ease, Tristan parried questions, prompting the villagers to speak of themselves. It worked every time. Almost.

A local with sparse stubble on his chin watched them in silence, and finally blurted out, "Bah! Can't fool me." He pushed himself to his feet. "You're here chasing those daft castle stories." He stomped out of the inn.

Tristan rubbed a hand down his short mustache and beard, fighting the urge to burst into laughter.

Another local regarded him with narrowed eyes. "Are you, then?"

"Nay," Tristan said. "Never heard of it till a week or two past."

"It seems to be the local sport," Cotrell said, "to gull travelers."

Snickers came from a group that had taken their ale to some benches by the fireplace.

"That may be," the local said, "but there is a castle."

"You've seen it, then?" Cotrell asked.

"Not I. Not fool enough to go get ripped up by those beasts down by the sea." He swung his legs over the bench. "And I'm not saying you are either. But there is a castle, all the same."

Tristan didn't even try to hide his grin. "Would that be the mysterious castle that fades out of sight in all but winter?"

The local stood as he scoffed. "That's just stories. The hills hide it, but it's there, all solid stone." He swung a woolen cloak around himself. "A shame that the beasts have solid fangs, as well." Then he, too, headed out into the night.

The matron humphed and slapped a tray down on the table. "Folly! All of it." She collected bowls and plates onto the tray. "'Tis wicked to convince young men to chase after nonsense that'll get 'em killed. The simple few that go, never come back. And what good would a locked-up, empty castle be to anyone, even if it weren't off in that lonely, wild forest?" She finished loading her tray and glared at them. "Tell me you're not chasin' off after that castle."

Tristan smiled at her. "Worry not."

TRISTAN TOSSED his pack to the head of a cot and dropped down beside it. The wood creaked as he stretched out, linking his hands behind his neck.

"How bad is the mattress?" James asked.

"Better than cold ground." Tristan cocked an eyebrow toward the rattling dormer window. "Particularly tonight."

"Indeed, my lord. 'Tis well we are out of that wind." James grasped one of Tristan's boots and drew it off, then the other.

A single oil lamp illuminated sparse furnishings under the sloped roof. By its light, James made quick notes in his pocket ledger, then set out morning gear beside the basin on the small table.

Cotrell came up the stairs from the silent common room. "All's well in the stable. The lad sleeps there when paying guests stay the night. Not a frequent occurrence, it would seem."

"By the talk round about," Tristan said, "I'd have thought they have a steady stream of castle-hunters passing through town."

"Not so. According to Toby, the terrible beasts keep travelers from heading west."

"What exactly *are* these terrible beasts?" James asked in his precise way.

Cotrell shed his jerkin. "Wolves, bears, and cats. All the more fearsome for lack of being seen." He hooked his jerkin on a peg. "My guess is that there are more of them in the unsettled woods.

The only other towns lie to the north and south, along the crossroad. Westbound, the road ends at a mill creek not far from here."

Trust Cotrell to already know more of their surroundings. 'Twas the reason Tristan had brought him on this mapping journey instead of his other two captains. "Have you noticed," Tristan asked, "how different the stories are in this town?"

James looked over his shoulder. "What mean you?"

"Elsewhere, the castle is spoken of as a rather mystical structure. The stuff of children's tales. Here, the castle's existence is a given. Even the beasts are not described in such gargantuan terms."

Cotrell stopped rummaging through his pack and regarded Tristan. "True enough."

"The question then, is *why*?"

"Could be any number of reasons," James said, pulling out the heavy nightshirt and cap he donned every eve. "Perhaps folk are less credulous here. What teases your interest now, when you've been laughing over it all along?" He turned. "If you'll hand me your jerkin, my lord."

Tristan sat up and shrugged the garment off into his waiting hands. "The odd specifics. Locked-up, for instance. An abandoned castle would be damaged, not sealed. Though, I suppose it makes little difference." He loosened the tie of his trousers for comfort and shook out the woolen blanket folded at the foot of his cot. "How far do you reckon we are from the sea, Cotrell?"

"Locals claim a distance anywhere from a week's journey to a month. All guesses, for none of them have ever been there. Besides, they don't have decent horses here. I've yet to see one in a running-walk. We can cover the ground faster."

Presently, James snuffed the lamp. Distant lightning flickered through the darkness. The glass rattled harder in its casement, accompanied by two sets of snores and pelting rain. Not that noise ever kept Tristan awake. So odd…those stories of an abandoned castle…

JAMES POURED hot water into the basin. "There'll be a hearty breakfast soon. Whipped eggs with chopped boar meat are in the oven. They make a fine cheese here too."

Tristan grunted and shed the rumpled shirt he'd slept in. He wiped himself down quickly before donning a fresh one, then splashed water over his face. He had to stoop to see his reflection in that faded excuse for a mirror. His black beard still made him look like a stranger to his own eyes.

He and Cotrell left James to his shaving and went down to enjoy the matron's skill again. She supplemented the baked eggs with a loaf of bread and a round of cheese, which he had little room for. Cotrell left the inn as James came down to break his fast.

Tristan finished his tea and rose from the table. "Buy the bread and cheese when you settle the tab."

"Aye, my l—" James clamped his lips.

At least no one was near to hear his mistake. Wondering what else James may have let slip, Tristan strode from the inn, past a pen of chickens, and into the stable.

"And I cleaned the tack too," Toby said to Cotrell. The lad's back was to the door, but when the stallion nickered, he swung around. "Good morn, sir. I did all that the horses could need, sir, save only that your stallion won't let me bridle him."

A laugh shook Tristan's chest, and he clapped a friendly hand onto the lad's shoulder. "Dauntless can be a bit stubborn."

"Aye, but not as bad as *some* stallions." Toby relaunched the list of all the tasks he'd completed.

Cotrell met Tristan's eye above Toby's head and gave him a quick nod, then grabbed Dauntless's bridle.

"Well done," Tristan said, handing the promised coin to the

lad. "You can help us saddle up. Put the pack harness on the gray."

Toby hurried to follow instructions. "Do you switch off which horse travels light?"

"Aye."

"You must be traveling far. Where are you heading?"

Tristan hid a smile, for the lad was even more direct than his elders. This time, he gave an answer he hadn't shared the night before. "Northwest, toward the River Thane."

"Ah! You *are* looking for the castle, then."

Tristan shook his head. "We seek the ridge crossing. Hard to tell where that may be unless we also know the woods on this side."

"What d'you need that for?"

"I heard from a friend who lives on the river that no one visits from the south anymore. I cannot help but wonder if something has closed the route."

Toby paused in buckling a strap. "You're not talking about the Lady Havella, are you?"

Tristan's brows twitched down. "Indeed, I am. Why do you speak so?" He hadn't meant it to, but his pitch had dropped.

Toby ducked his head and pulled on the buckle. "I meant no disrespect, sir. Just surprised."

"Ah." Tristan resumed his casual tone. "Why surprised?"

"Uh...guess I don't know the particulars. Just heard she...she doesn't let people come anymore. Not poor ones, anyway. But I don't know much about that, so I shouldn't speak out."

"Hm."

Toby cast a sideways glance at him. "Uh, do you want to take a little feed on your journey? We could spare some oats."

That was a stretch. Anxious to get back on Tristan's good side, it seemed. He smiled at Toby. "Nay, but you can give them a handful now."

Toby scooped some from a small barrel and offered it to the

gray, while Cotrell raised his brows at Tristan and moved on to saddle another horse.

Dauntless snorted and stamped.

Chuckling, Tristan brought him some oats. "Your manners lack polish."

Toby wiped his hands on his trousers. "If you're going over the ridge...well, for one thing, be on the watch for the bears and wolves, but..." He glanced away and back again. "Why would you risk that, and not look for the castle too?"

Tristan stepped back from the stallion's searching nose. "Would you have me wander over every unmapped hill, hoping to find a castle beyond the next? Snow will fly before we find it."

Toby shrugged. "Yesterday was chilly, but the wind scarce comes out of the north. There'll be plenty of fair days yet. What if..." He swallowed and whispered, "What if you knew where to look?"

Tristan raised an eyebrow. "If I could know that, surely others could have known it before me."

Toby shook his head and kept his voice low. "My gra'pa Burk lived there when he was a boy. He would never tell where it was. Said it wasn't ours and stealing from nobles could end with hanging. But now...well, he mutters about them never coming back. A couple weeks ago, I heard him arguing with my ma and pa. I have good ears, better than most, anyway. My ma cried and said she'd never forgive him if I ran off searching."

Toby looked down. "I'm their only child, you see, and well...I love our farm. I can't go, even if I wanted to. But it seems an awful waste, that castle stands there empty."

Tristan considered the lad. "Why tell me? A stranger. Why not one of your friends?"

"Pa says nobody in town will be anyone's friend if they all go mad after the castle." He shrugged. "I guess it used to be trouble, even back when my pa was little. But you don't live here. You're rich, and I heard the other one call you 'lord,' so you must be a noble."

Behind Toby, Cotrell shook his head.

Tristan kept a still face as Toby rambled on. "My gra'pa says the town was bigger and people had fine things when the nobles used the castle. There was even a school here. Maybe it will help the whole town if nobles lived there again." He paused and looked hopefully up at Tristan. "It won't do to tell anyone where you're bound, but our farm lies north of the mill. Just follow the lane along this side of the creek. I can run ahead crosswise through the woods and meet you there. Tell my gra'pa about you."

Tristan opened his mouth, but Toby startled and hissed, "Someone's coming."

Toby grabbed one of the saddled horses and led it out of the stable. Sure enough, the innkeeper and James were crossing the yard toward them.

Tristan led the gray out and handed the reins to James. "Just bring them around front, and we'll load up."

In the foreyard, James stared at him as Tristan inspected the provisions, then sent the innkeeper for more cheese and dried meat. Indeed, 'twas hard to move this slow, but the lad, loping off beyond a broken-down cottage, needed a head start. A cup of strong tea added a few more minutes, then they mounted and left town.

"What was all that about?" James asked.

Tristan smiled down at him, for the bay mare made him seem even shorter than he was. "The lad Toby, or perhaps his grandfather, seems to know a few more things about the castle than most."

"What is that to us?"

Tristan's lips twitched. "Haven't you always chided me for excessive curiosity?"

James closed his eyes and released a breath.

Laughter crept into Tristan's voice. "As it happens, Toby is arranging for us to visit his grandfather. 'Twould be rude to ignore the invitation now."

From behind, Cotrell asked, "What do you suppose he meant about the Lady Havella?"

"That was odd." Tristan's frown deepened. "I can't imagine her turning anyone away. Certainly, no one from Moorelin. It makes no sense that she'd treat folk different on this side of the river."

James demanded an explanation, and Cotrell told him of the conversation while they followed the poorly kept road. At least the sun was drying the mud.

"Strange," James said when Cotrell finished, "but there have always been rumors. 'Tis bound to happen with a lady such as she. More so, considering the waters of Fountain Isle. But why tell Toby we're looking for a route over the ridge?"

"I just wanted to keep him talking about the lay of the westward land," Tristan said. "'Twas only a passing comment from the lady that I made use of."

"How long ago did she tell you that?" Cotrell asked.

Tristan shrugged. "I haven't been to Fountain Isle in three years. May have even been the time before that."

They found the lane as they descended a hill toward a gurgling steam. Nothing more than a rutted cart track, forcing them to ride single file. Branches clacked overhead, the storm having stripped most of the fading leaves. Beyond a curve, Toby awaited them outside a tiny cottage. A larger cottage and barn were visible through the trees.

"I told my gra'pa about you," Toby said as they dismounted. He looked worried. "'Tis not one of his better days, but he said the lord could come in."

Tristan followed Toby, ducking his head to pass through the low doorway. The reek of wild tobacco stung his nose. A fire burned on the stone hearth, and a man sat beside it, only his bald head visible above the blanket that wrapped him. Furnishings were few but looked to be well crafted.

Tristan moved around to face him, for Toby was already saying, "Gra'pa Burk, this is the nobleman I told you of."

Watery eyes looked up at him, from amidst countless wrinkles in sallow skin.

"I am Lord Tristan," he said, omitting his family name. He bowed slightly to the man's advanced age.

Burk wheezed as he stared. "You're not one of them. They were fair."

What did that mean? Did his mind wander? This could be difficult. Tristan lowered himself to the chair opposite the old man. "Of whom do you speak?"

"The master and mistress!" he snarled, as though that were a fool's question.

"Of the castle," Toby added, as his grandfather burst into coughing.

"Ah. Certain, I could not look like them. My family has never held land here. We dwell north of the River Thane."

Burk's brown-spotted hand pulled the blanket tighter. "At least ye don't come with lies." He heaved a wheezy sigh, head sagging forward. "All lost. Such beauty...given over to those foul beasts."

More rambling. "Can you tell me the names of the master and mistress?" Tristan asked.

"Names? Nay. I was but a lad, not half Toby's age." His gaze grew distant. "Oh, but she was a fine lady. Golden locks coiled around her head. A smile bright as the sun."

"What was the master like?"

"Well enough, I suppose, though he didn't smile unless his lady was near." Burk brought his gaze back to Tristan. "Why think ye that I would know much of them? Our place was beside the stable."

This meandering didn't seem to suit Toby. "But, Gra'pa, you know more about the castle than anyone, for your papa was caretaker. First in and last out. You could tell of that."

"Aye, he was. My papa loaded us all up in the spring...so we could get the castle ready for the family. And when they left, we'd pack once more. Mama'd lead the donkey out so Papa could close up the gates." He sagged again. "Until they didn't come. We waited and waited. The castle's mournful silent without the family." He shook his head. "But such a din all night. Mama couldn't bear the howls. They'd gotten so fierce we could barely sleep, so we left after mid-summer night."

A rugged cough interrupted. Burk wiped his lips on the blanket. "Mama feared to come back the next spring. Papa said we'd wait for the family to come through town...and journey with them. But they never did. Papa even went alone to check the castle...in case they'd taken the low route that spring. But it stood empty."

"Did they send word?"

Burk shook his head. "Don't think they could've. My papa kept hoping and worrying both. Afraid someone would rob the castle, which he was bound to keep. He'd locked up the gates, and none but he knew the hidden way. But still he fretted." Burk cleared his throat. "Told us we couldn't speak of the castle at all. Except the beasts. He talked about them, and Mama did too. Dreadful scared, she was, and glad to stay near town. Believed the beasts had gotten the family, she did. Mayhap she was right, but Papa didn't believe it."

"Why not?"

"Don't know. Can't see what else it could've been. Those vixicat yowls still sound in my dreams. Fiercest beasts there ever was! No one dared leave the castle at night, nor go down the western valley, even in daylight."

Vixicat? Never had Tristan heard of such a creature. "What does a vixicat look like?"

Burk sneered. "No one lives to tell." He glowered a moment. "I used to walk the castle walls with my papa that last summer... but we never caught sight of one in the dusk. The castle sits atop a cliff on the sunset side. My papa would lift me up to look over the parapet, but I could see naught but the treetops."

Finally, a reference to the land. "How far from here to the cliff?"

"Never counted the days bouncing along in that cart."

"You camped in the woods along the way, then?"

"Aye. My papa standing by the fire with his bow when I slept...my mama bearing it when I woke."

Tristan questioned further, discovered where the road left town, but not the route, save that the ridge could be seen along the first part of the trek.

"Can you not see the ridge from the castle?" Tristan asked.

"Nay, the hills get in the way. And the ravine, though that stretches a long way down toward the sea. Vixicat land, Papa said." Burk faded off again, the mournful look returning. "Terrible sad to think of those beasts tearing up that fine lady." A long wheeze escaped him. "At least there's someone else to remember them now. Lifts a burden, it does."

Tristan stood. "I'm glad of that. Thank you for sharing your memories with me."

Another coughing fit overwhelmed Burk's answer.

Tristan left the cottage quietly.

Toby followed, looking downcast. "I'm sorry, sir. I thought he'd know more than that."

Tristan put a hand on his shoulder. "That's not your fault. How old is your grandfather?"

"Some ways past seventy. He doesn't like us to count his years."

"Memories can fade in seventy years."

Toby broke a dead branch sticking out from a nearby tree trunk and snapped it in half. "I don't see why people keep secrets. If they're so important, they shouldn't be lost. But that's what happens."

There was more to Toby then met the eye. "You have a good point."

They stopped by the horses, and Toby looked up at him. "Why do you keep secrets? Why don't you tell that you're a lord?"

Young enough to be naive, but old enough to ask serious

questions. "Because folk make too much of titles in these parts. I'm the youngest son, so I cannot pass my title on. I am who I am, whether anyone calls me lord."

"Do you want me to keep it secret too?"

"You needn't speak of it without cause, but don't think I am asking you to lie if the question arises." Toby looked relieved, and Tristan mounted Dauntless. "You'll make a fine man, Toby Burk. Thank you for bringing me to meet your grandfather."

CHAPTER 2

In the Border Lands

Tristan led the way back along the lane. He turned toward the creek, then followed it north until they found a place to cross. The horses splashed through, and a bit farther on, Tristan paused by a broken, weathered timber protruding from the bank.

Cotrell noticed it too, his eyes tracing the hard earth on both sides of the creek and scanning the woods westward. "There must have been a bridge here."

"I take it you heard what the elder Burk said."

He nodded, still studying the woods. "I lingered by the door. Can't imagine how you stood it inside. Whatever he puts in his pipe should be buried far from town."

"In*deed*!" Tristan let his horse amble forward. "Where did the road lie?"

"I will guess, up through there." Cotrell pointed northwest. "Don't expect to track it far."

"Why does it matter?" James asked.

Tristan turned Dauntless back toward the others and patted his neck. "It will take us within view of the ridge and give us a reference point."

The dip in James's pitch was almost imperceptible. "I thought we were looking for a plain that would lead us down to the sea."

Tristan's shoulders shook with silent laughter. "I heard that, James. The part you didn't say."

Cotrell grinned, but answered James, "I was told the plain is narrow, and I don't know where it begins. The height will help us understand the whole, so we can find the parts."

"Don swords and bows," Tristan said, reaching to unhook his quiver and wrist guard from the pack horse. "We'll ride northwest."

They reached the crest of the ridge some hours after noon. Tristan sat atop the cliff, gazing out over the wide River Thane. Dozens of times, he had looked up from below, but never had he surveyed the valley from above. His homeland was but a faint blur northeast across the river. To the west, the black peak of Fountain Isle should thrust up from the mighty river. Yet even with his long vision, he could not make it out. He looked up at Cotrell, who was turning in a slow circle, doubtless committing all to memory. "What think you? Could you place us on our map?"

"A guess only, and I can add *nothing* south of the ridge," Cotrell grumbled. "This forest stretches forever, it seems, with no landmark in view. I can't even tell if we've passed beyond Verenlia's uncertain border."

"By now, we must have." Tristan swung his legs around and accepted Cotrell's grip to pull him to his feet. "I even doubt the last few towns owe allegiance to any noble, much less a king."

"Why?"

"Verenlian nobility think too much of their own rank to let it go unnoticed on their lands. We no longer saw their colors nor heard their names."

"Are we nearing Lavaycia, then?" James asked.

"Nay. It has to be beyond that plain we seek, though I'm not sure how far." Tristan made a vague gesture southward. "I just know that the road to it heads southwest farther down Verenlia's border." He turned and took a last glance over the northern vista. "Let's get down out of this wind."

They snacked on bread and cheese, then led their horses for a time, while Tristan told James what little he'd learned in the cottage. Finding a meager stream, they let the horses drink.

Cotrell pointed to some tracks. "A fair number of deer, but I've yet to see wolf or bear."

"I suspect those stories are overstated," Tristan said. "What man brings his family twice a year though a horde of ferocious beasts?" He drank from his waterskin. "And though they kept watch through the night, he also braved a lone ride to the castle and back."

Cotrell knelt to refill the waterskins. "Nor did he believe that beasts killed *the family*, whomever they may have been."

"That would be a stretch, indeed," James said. "Doubtless, they traveled with servants and men-at-arms."

"Aye, they would have." Tristan passed a rein over Dauntless's neck. "With two routes, it seems unlikely that anyone here would know how the family fared on the trip to their winter home." He mounted. "Any number of things could have interfered with the spring journey. Burk's father set out as usual, so he must have suspected nothing." Tristan frowned as he waited. "What later caused folk to believe they were killed? And if true, when, where, and why?"

Cotrell was last to mount. "'Tis a pity," he said, "that the only witness was a child at the time."

"Aye, and he's not long for this world." Tristan settled into the rhythm of his horse's stride.

"An intriguing mystery," James said, "but after seventy years, we aren't likely to solve it."

They paralleled the ridge, and near sunset, Cotrell ascended to its crest again, this time taking the map to mark their location. Tristan found level ground, with a rock outcropping to shield one side, and began setting up camp with James.

When Cotrell returned, he and Tristan spread the map against the rock. Cotrell tapped the ridge line drawn on the parchment. "I place us about here."

"We're still along the part that is inaccessible from the northern side," Tristan murmured.

"Aye." Cotrell pointed to another spot. "Over here is the first possibility of scaling the ridge from the north, although still too steep for a wagon. A couple days' ride, at our current pace."

"Hm." Tristan rolled the map and fed it into the leather tube that Cotrell held. Nearby, the horses shredded vegetation, a discordant sound in the quiet woods. Tristan stared at them for a moment. "Let's water these greedy beasts. There's a spring not far."

While the horses drank, Cotrell studied the ground. "Some wolves ran through here...sometime after the rain stopped." He took a few more steps. "Heading southeast. Moving fast. Hopefully, they took their prey down. I prefer sated wolves to hungry ones."

"And did they leave enormous footprints?"

Cotrell chuckled. "Hate to disappoint, but they are on the ordinary side."

James had a fire going when they returned. Dinner and beds were far less desirable than last night, but at least it didn't rain. Cotrell tossed his weighted line over a convenient branch and hoisted their supplies beyond the reach of any bear, while Tristan picked a spot and settled down with his bow for the first watch of the night.

WHEN TRISTAN AWOKE the next morn, James had the fire ready for cooking. He did not stand a watch, never having learned to handle a bow nor any steel beyond his long dagger. Instead, he rose with the dawn and attended to water, meals, clothing, and a host of small tasks. The only drawback to this well-organized camp was that it reminded Tristan of battle days.

Not memories he cherished, especially when cold, hungry, and stiff. He pushed himself off the hard ground, stretched, and after a brief walk in the woods, sat down by the fire. Bacon sizzled, making his mouth water and stomach rumble.

Cotrell tore a third off the last of the bread and passed the rest to Tristan. "Where shall we head, my lord? West along the ridge, or strike out south, hoping to find that plain?"

"The ridge."

"Why?" James asked, accepting his portion of bread from Tristan.

"Partly, because I keep puzzling over Toby's remark about the Lady Havella. If the crossing is blocked, that may shed some light. If it is not blocked, it could save us a good deal of time getting home, but only if we know where it is. We may need it if the weather takes an unexpected turn."

James looked at the blue sky. "Today will be warm. Winter is yet a ways off."

"Our hostess at the inn said that 'the simple few that go, never return.'" Tristan narrowed his eyes over those cryptic words. "If the beasts are exaggerated, what kills the searchers? The tales describe a castle that can only be seen in winter. Bare trees, perhaps." He swept a hand toward branches above. "Which makes me think of these. Cold can kill, and no sword or bow can defeat it. Might there be winter storms blowing in off the sea? We of Moorelin know nothing of coastal weather."

They struck camp and set off. The forest gradually changed to pine. Ancient trunks with green tufts perched high above. The lower branches had long since broken away, leaving more room for the riders. They covered the needle-strewn ground in the smooth running-walk of Moorelin's finely bred horses.

To his left, Tristan could make out broad-leaf trees farther down the slope, but ahead, the pines stretched so far that nothing could be seen between them, except more trunks. The silence of the forest blended into an uncanny mix of peaceful and lonely. Welcome, in a way, after the pretentious cities of Verenlia.

How quickly he had tired of them. Their excitement seemed a façade. He preferred the cities of Moorelin after all, though their familiarity wore on him. Not that he didn't love his land and his family. There was just nothing left for the youngest of five sons to do.

Now, at least. Not so, a year ago. Vicious skirmishes on Moorelin's northeastern border had consumed his days—and many nights. Just thinking about it made his pulse quicken. The war bellows of the Graybonite raiders echoed in memory. The screams of terror, the burning cottages, the ache of exhausted muscles, the body of his friend...

Tristan exhaled and released his futile grip on his sword hilt. Stretching his fingers, he called on later memories, when he and his archers had finally driven the Graybonites back across the border. And the day that Captain Cotrell had reported back with his band of scouts...the raiding nomads had set off toward their northern lands. 'Twould be a generation before the tribe ventured near again. How they had celebrated that night! The dances of warriors and the triple-cheers of *morrah*. Tristan patted Dauntless's neck. Even he had frisked in the lazy days that followed.

For a time, having nothing to do was pure bliss. But empty days...Tristan shook his head...how soon they bred boredom. His brother had sent him off to maintain their family's relations with Verenlia. Or so he said, perhaps to make it sound important. In truth, a short visit was adequate. Tristan stretched it into a tour, desperate for activity. 'Twas a godsend that he had chanced to notice an odd gap on their maps.

So here he wandered—mapping uncharted lands. An endeavor no one had requested. Precious little value in it. Moorelin had no interest in this land. Even the location of the ridge crossing mattered little—provided all was well with the Lady Havella. And it probably was. She had a guard, after all. The biggest man Tristan had ever seen. With only one access point to Fountain Isle, that guard wouldn't be easily overpowered.

The hours of riding through empty forest grew tiresome. Endlessly guiding a horse and watching the unremarkable woods. Why could he never get past this restless feeling? The cities were too brash, the woods too quiet. Too many people, not enough people. What did he want? Where did he belong? He glowered. So far into his third decade—certain, he should know by now.

"Hold," Cotrell said. He stopped, looked all around, then walked his horse several paces aside. A fox darted away with a bone in its jaws. Cotrell studied the ground, his bow in hand as always, then rejoined them. "Another deer kill, with little left for the scavengers. The wolves may not be oversized, but there are a great many."

"Plenty of game means plenty of wolves," Tristan said.

"True."

They set off again. The near side of the ridge grew steeper as they traveled, forcing them to ride farther from the peak. Nonetheless, they scaled it twice a day to track their position against northern landmarks. They made camp, then repeated it all the next day, and the next.

The rolling hills descended overall, and cedars joined the forest. Bear tracks interspersed the wolves', and by the fifth day, they were indeed larger.

"Not entirely surprising," James said. "There is usually a little seed of truth behind grand tales."

Cotrell grunted. "I'm still wondering about the vixicats. I've seen only one set of cat prints, and they were no bigger than a fox's print. A small lynx, perhaps."

"Burk's description placed vixicats west of the castle," Tristan said, scanning the forest. "Wherever that might be." The rising sun angled across the slope to their right. "What think you of this ascent, Cotrell?"

"More promising than most. Shall we ride up?"

"Aye."

They gained the crest. At last—a possible crossing. A few trees and enough soil to support grass ran along the top for fifty yards or so.

Tristan studied the valley as the horses grazed. Grassland stretched in a long swath beside the river below. A lone cart traveled east from the distant peak of Fountain Isle, following the south shore. 'Twas the only route, for the bridge to the isle lay on this side of the River Thane. He joined Cotrell, and they looked for a descent route on the river-facing side of the ridge.

Cotrell shook his head. "Still too steep and rocky."

Tristan gripped a small tree and leaned outward. Pointing west, he said, "It looks better over there. Let's continue."

Boulders forced them to descend again, but around noon, they reached the crest on a gradual ascent. A high meadow stretched twenty to thirty feet wide and a hundred yards long, with few boulders jutting through the grass.

Higher ground rose to the west, and James pointed up it. "Look, my lord. A stream."

"Excellent! And good fortune this high. We'll lunch here." Tristan dismounted. "Walk with me, Cotrell."

They paced the meadow and found two piles of small boulders, which flanked smooth ground that descended the north slope. Success warmed Tristan's chest. "Cleared of rocks and easily the width of a carriage. That, my friend, was once a road."

Cotrell followed the slope a few paces and smiled up at him. "Aye, this must be it."

He stomped grass aside to find the direction of the road, while Tristan let his gaze linger on Fountain Isle, closer now, but still northwest of their position.

The river frothed around the long island. Lush on this end, with a black peak jutting high at the far end. He could just make out the spacious cottage that stood on the island. No sign of any disruption, but how could he really tell from here? There had been a couple instances over the decades when unscrupulous folk had ousted the Lady Havella from her domain and tried to extort a profit from those desperate for the waters.

As Tristan watched, a tiny dark figure came into view, crossing in front of the cottage. That had to be the same guard. Few men were tall enough to make that cottage look small.

Cotrell returned up the bit of old road he'd exposed and followed Tristan's gaze. "Looks peaceful to me. Does your long vision tell you anything I cannot see?"

Tristan shrugged. "I saw a tall man stroll a few paces. By height, he is likely the same guard."

Cotrell lifted his brows and glanced back at the distant isle. "The things you can see never cease to amaze me."

"I feel much the same when you tell me of something you heard. Let's see if we can find the southbound road."

They discovered a likely spot more toward the western end of the meadow, where James was setting out food on a flat rock. Instead of grass, trees had encroached on this slope, making it harder to find the road.

Tristan noticed some bare, blackened trunks, and he climbed a tilted slab of rock to look over the edge. A burnt, split trunk remained below the black scar, now carpeted with foot-tall pines.

Cotrell joined him. "It must have been hit by lightning, soon followed by rain, for it didn't burn much of the woods." He narrowed his eyes at the lowest trunk. "That must have been one ancient tree."

Tristan considered the distant view, staring through the gap left by the fire. "I fancy I see sparkling blue on the horizon, and

I think there is a bare swath between this forest and that farthest, hazy rise." He sucked in a breath, a tingle coursing up to his scalp. He snapped his arm straight and pointed across the hills. "Look!"

"What do you see?" Cotrell shaded his eyes. "Is it within my range?"

"I believe so. Is that not a peaked tower roof, just barely showing through the highest branches? Ah, there is another beyond it. Roofed in blue tiles."

"Towers, indeed!" Cotrell exclaimed.

Tristan tilted his head back and laughed. "We have found the castle!"

James hurried over. Cotrell jumped down and gave him a leg up onto the rough perch.

A little more exclaiming, and then James said, "Now that we've found it, let's eat."

He scooted down the rock face, and Tristan jumped to level ground. "Ah, James! Ever practical."

Tristan said little as they consumed a dull meal, but his gaze turned southwest ever and again.

Cotrell cast sideways looks toward him, then slid a question out, excessively casual. "I wonder which direction we'll head next."

Tristan laughed. "If you think I'm going to pass up a close look at that mysterious castle, you are not the captain who has followed me these last few years."

Cotrell grinned.

A moment passed before James said, "'Tis not without risk."

"Nothing is without risk," Tristan said. "We intended to cross over to the plain anyway, and then down to the sea, so it's really not even a detour. We can reach the castle before dusk and give the horses a day to rest while we...*investigate*." He couldn't help laughing again, for even to his own ears, boyish mischief infused his words. And, oh, it felt good! "Let's plan."

He and Cotrell climbed to the perch again, counted hills, and agreed on a route, while James packed up. Down the old road, they headed, losing it at times and finding it again, until a sharp drop-off brought them to a dead stop. A cascading stream had cut a deep cleft between the hills. Hewn timbers, rotted and broken, hung down the opposite side.

CHAPTER 3

Beyond the Border Lands

The three men looked down the chasm, their eyes tracing it east and west.

Tristan's stomach felt leaden. "Too far to jump," he said. "We'll have to find a crossing."

Cotrell's voice lowered. "If someone bothered to build a bridge, there is no nearby crossing."

Tristan shifted his legs, and Dauntless backed. "We've had good travels all along. There is bound to be something that does not favor us. Hence, we adjust our plan. Which direction do you suggest?"

Cotrell sat still, but Tristan knew he was not inactive. Listening, rather, to the myriad rustles throughout the woods and testing the breeze. Finally, he said, "East."

They turned their mounts, following the chasm, which remained deep. Slow going amidst the trees. The pack horse stumbled but recovered. Though James kept it near, leading a horse through rugged woods proved troublesome. Farther up the hill, a large stag watched them with statuesque poise. A couple of does raised their heads behind it, then returned to eating.

The men continued searching, for they had no other choice. From the corner of his eye, Tristan glimpsed a gray form rising from an equally gray outcropping. Half again as big as any wolf should be.

"Cotrell," he whispered, drawing an extra arrow from his quiver.

They stopped at the same instant. "Yes, I saw it. There is another. James, turn and retrace. Do *not* run."

It took James a moment to turn both horses. Slowly, they moved back the way they had come.

The wolves slunk down into the undergrowth, following. Another joined them. Probably more hidden from view. Tristan spotted the stag again but kept his eyes averted. It was fixated on the horses.

Let it stay that way!

Guiding Dauntless with only his knees, he held one arrow nocked and the other ready. Through his legs, Tristan felt Dauntless's tension, but battle-trained, the horse would never bolt.

They passed below the deer. Not much longer. Hoofbeats measured the passing seconds. Then, behind him, the sharp snap of Cotrell's bow. The stag leapt—off balance—an arrow in its shoulder. The does fled up the ridge. The stag blundered, gaining speed as it followed them. With the call of a single wolf, the pack burst from cover and pursued the stag.

"Steady on," Cotrell said.

In a few minutes, thrashing in the woods told of the certain ending.

Tristan exhaled, his next breath feeling fresh and new. He motioned Cotrell forward and murmured, "Well done. Lead."

Cotrell, on his gray, moved ahead of James. Tristan's heart returned to a calmer rhythm. They passed the broken bridge and continued on.

Jagged slabs of rock tilted from the forest floor, forcing them to ride farther from the stream. They paused to confer. James's expression remained calm, but his fist gripped the reins tighter than needed.

Cotrell looked grim, his searching eyes never still. "We lost over an hour backtracking."

"Do you still have a feel for the direction of the castle?" Tristan asked, not that he doubted it.

"South-southwest," Cotrell replied.

"We were fortunate, back there," James said, "that deer were nearby. What if we are chased again?"

"If we can protect our backs," Tristan said, "a few well-placed arrows will drive off wolves." He nodded toward the bay mare, their pack horse today. "If not, release her lead and stay ahead of her." Sad, but better to sacrifice a horse than any of them. Tristan took the map tube from the pack and buckled it to his saddle. They each transferred some necessities to their own horses.

Cotrell raised his head. "Hush!" After a moment, he said, "There are a couple of bears a good way off. They seem to be occupied with an argument."

"Let's not wait for them to finish." Tristan nudged Dauntless with his knees and headed south, hoping to reach the stream again. What had become of it? Had it veered away?

Any hope of recovering lost time was soon dashed. They could never see far enough ahead to avoid obstacles. Game trails led around them, but wolf prints were almost as plentiful as deer. Then, they saw the bear tracks. The *size* of them!

Cotrell's brows stayed high as he looked from the ground to Tristan. "We shouldn't have laughed at those stories."

Time and again, they had to backtrack for one cause or another. As the sun sank, they rounded a hill, hoping to follow the valley south. Instead, they found that a rotted tree had tipped down the steep slope, crushing the smaller trees below into an impassable tangle.

At least they hadn't gone far along this blocked path. They found another route, though not south.

Cotrell pointed at tracks. "A bear headed east here not long ago."

They turned west and found a broader valley with the sun slanting through it.

"We cannot follow this for long," Cotrell said, "but 'tis a relief to be able to see ahead for a change."

"Indeed." Tristan looked at the sky. Wind rattled the gold-flecked branches farther up the hills and filtered through the valley. "I don't see us reaching the castle before nightfall."

"Nor do I." Cotrell halted his gray gelding. "Though the moon is nearing full, I've no fancy to wander these woods by its light alone."

"'Twould be madness," James said. "Let us find a site to make camp."

The best they could find was shielded by steep hills on the north and south. Tristan tied his stallion beside the mare on the west side, and Cotrell tied the other two horses on the east.

As the men gathered wood, a distant yowl brought all three upright. Tristan and Cotrell dropped their armloads and slipped their bows from shoulder to hand. They made not a sound, listening to the answering yowl. The beasts could not be near, but the way their calls increased, lifted the hair on the back of Tristan's neck. They reached a crescendo and erupted into fierce battle. In the end, only one deep-throated beast was left yowling of its victory.

Cotrell drew an audible breath. "I take that to be a vixicat."

"Aye," Tristan said, his voice low. "Keep your bow up, Cotrell. James and I will gather the wood, and plenty of it."

Two more fights echoed through the forest as Tristan stood the first watch and fed the fire to keep a steady blaze. Occasional snores murmured during the lulls, but he doubted his friends slept well.

When the moon passed its zenith, the woods had been still

for perhaps an hour. Tristan found it harder to stay awake. He circled the fire, then leaned against a tree. Dauntless and the mare grew restless, and the other two horses angled their ears westward.

Tristan could hear nothing but the shifting horses. He slipped the toe of his boot under Cotrell's shoulder and nudged him.

Cotrell grunted and rolled to his side, mumbling, "My turn?"

"Get up."

The horses stamped and tugged at their reins. In an instant, Cotrell was on his feet, bow in hand. James cast aside his cloak and drew his dagger. All else was quiet.

Try as he might, Tristan could see nothing. Keeping his back to the fire, he took a step closer to Dauntless, bow half drawn. Something must be out there. If only he could—

A flurry of breaking branches erupted. The mare tried to flee, then reared, snapping the branch she was tied to. Black jaws clamped on her neck.

Dauntless kicked. A solid thud, which changed nothing.

The beast shook the mare violently, dragging it backward.

Tristan snapped out of shock and shot his arrow. He and Cotrell peppered the creature with arrows as it turned and dragged the horse away. The clamor in the woods slowly faded into the distance.

His heart thudded through an eternity. Beside him, Cotrell panted. Tristan's pulse finally began to slow, and his stomach revolted. After a moment, he wiped his mouth, then went to calm Dauntless, smoothing a hand down his sweaty neck.

Several minutes passed before any of them spoke. Cotrell tossed more wood onto the fire.

James, his voice still unsteady, asked, "How big was that thing exactly?"

"I don't know," Tristan said. "Bigger than a horse."

"It stank worse than a bear," Cotrell grumbled. "How clear of a look did you get?"

"Not very." Tristan spread his hands apart. "Its jaws must have been this long. Narrow, like a fox's snout, but its eyes were gold and...cat-like." He dwelt on the image seared into his mind. "Its teeth were wrong."

"Wrong, how?" Cotrell asked.

Tristan shook his head. "Too many of them, or maybe just strangely placed. I had no time to inspect them."

"True," Cotrell murmured. "It doesn't mind arrows. I'm sure we hit it at least a dozen times. I made out a couple arrows as it turned, but they hadn't gone deep. At that range, the shafts ought to have penetrated."

Silence lengthened.

"Now what?" James asked.

"Only two choices, in this moment," Tristan replied. "We either ride or stay. Your opinion, Cotrell?"

"That beast will be too busy gorging to bother us tonight, but there could be others. The last thing I want is to ride unfamiliar woods with black night-hunters on the prowl."

"Agreed." Tristan looked at the pack they'd hoisted up a tree. "Let's divide that up and leave what we don't absolutely require. Get the horses ready to ride in case we must, then we'll stand watch till first light."

THIS THEY DID, reaching the stream again as the sun rose. At long last, they descended a steep hill and found a crossing.

The horses struggled up the opposite bank. Either skirting or climbing each new obstacle, they eventually found a grassy hilltop where an aged maple spread fat limbs.

Cotrell climbed up into it and scanned their surroundings. He looked down at Tristan. "I'm tired of your yawning, so here is the plan. James and I will keep watch from the boughs in opposite directions. You sleep at the base. If anything approaches, we'll wake you, and you may scamper up the tree like a squirrel."

Tristan accorded that a weak smile and didn't bother arguing.

After a nap and some dried meat, Tristan climbed high through the branches and found the blue-peaked towers again. "'Tis due south," he said, settling on the limb beside Cotrell, where they could scan the hilltops. "Let's choose our route."

James strapped a pouch to a saddle. "Why are we still chasing that castle, when we have discovered that the stories of the beasts are true?"

"'Tis still between us and the plain," Tristan said. "Assuming it has at least some walls intact, we'll be able to get a decent night's sleep."

"Is that the only reason?"

"Trust me, James, I am as put off by the neighbors as you are. Nonetheless, I would understand what is here. The route, Cotrell."

They soon set out over the hills again, maintaining constant vigilance and taking note of the tracks and scat. Rabbits, foxes, deer, a few small lynx, and southward, some wild boar. Unfortunately, wolves seemed to infest the area, all oversized. And the bear tracks…Tristan did *not* want to meet one. They came close once, almost stumbling on a gaping hole in a hillside, with scored tree trunks on the slope below it. At least that was the only time they needed to alter their route, for the hills rolled more gently with wider valleys and less strenuous climbs.

James said little, making it all the more startling when he halted and declared, "That's a walnut tree."

Tristan blinked and followed the direction of his pointing finger. They spent hours watching for dangerous beasts…and he pointed out a *tree?*

Cotrell drawled, "'That's not in attack posture. No need to worry."

James turned a scornful look on Cotrell, while Tristan leaned over his horse's neck, shaking in silent laughter. He curtailed it as quick as he could, for James always had a reason. "A walnut, you say. How do you know?"

"'Tis the sort of thing I learned when I trained with your father's steward. They are useful for food."

Did such a tree occur naturally, or did this mean something more? Tristan scanned amidst the treetops, but too many still clung to their golden canopy. He touched a heel to his horse's flank and picked up the pace.

Cresting the hill, he drew rein, his pulse quickening at the sight that met his eyes.

CHAPTER 4

Lavaycia

Four cousins gathered at the back of Maerton Castle's hall, each from a different house of Lavaycia.

Beth motioned the other three near and whispered, "This is our chance. Let's escape to the woods."

"Just us," Ivan said, somewhere between question and demand.

She knew he meant just her and him, but said, "Aye, the four of us." She took Sareen's hand and turned for the rear doors.

Servants reached them first and opened the double doors. Ivan and Layton followed the ladies down the terrace steps and across the formal gardens.

Ivan took the place at her side. His brown hair smelled of the pomade he used to hold it in place. Always sensitive that one of his eyes sat slightly higher than the other, he masked the flaw with a fixed sweep of hair across his brow. A shame that he was touchy. Oddities were common enough.

Beth followed the shortest route to the hunting gate. Until

they were beyond that barrier, it was all too likely that they would be summoned to return. As though there was any purpose in watching Lavaycia's elder nobility strut their dignified selves about Maerton's grand hall.

Her mother's words came to mind. *You are old enough to participate.* 'Twas true only if *participate* meant to be seen. Certain, no one wanted to hear Beth's voice!

Ivan took the lead and hailed the gatekeeper. "Open!"

Doubtless, he would be good at strutting when he inherited his father's title and lands.

The gatekeeper complied with the imperious demand, and they soon passed the gate.

Behind her, Layton spoke to a guard. "Should any inquire, we are..."

She hurried on, not wanting to hear him tell their whereabouts, even though his forethought might lessen the reprimand she'd endure later. If her father knew where she was, and that she had proper escort, he would perhaps tolerate her slipping away.

The trampled earth gave way to forest floor. A cool breeze swept around her neck, and she wished she could let her hair down. At least the sleeves of her mint-green gown were long. Fallen leaves rustled beneath their feet. Paths meandered between the bare trunks. Unnecessary, for the woods were groomed for hunting. Plenty of room to run horses between trees and thickets.

A falling red leaf settled into Sareen's black curls as she turned onto a path. 'Twas her way to take the prescribed course.

As a lady should, echoed within Beth. Why must she always hear her mother's voice even when she was a day's journey away?

Beth pushed the thought away and spread her hands to the breeze. "Ah, we used to run all through these woods," she said. "Let this be our day of remembrance."

Sareen wrinkle her child-like nose. "What mean you?"

"No titles between us four today." Beth spun to give her smile to each of them. "Just our simple names."

"How unkind you are to Layton," Ivan said. "He just got his bestowed title of *sir*, and now you want to take it away from him."

True to form, Ivan uttered *sir* with a faint hiss, turning her companionable words to a barb. Even when she asked it of him, he couldn't resist pointing out the obvious fact that he outranked Layton. 'Twas on the tip of her tongue to state another obvious fact, for Ivan hated it. Nay, the lady within her could no longer stoop to that bickering. Ugh!

"Speak not of any titles," Sareen said. "We are cousin-friends, as we have always been."

Dear Sareen. Ever willing to follow Beth's lead. The closest thing Beth had to a sister. Sareen launched into a dramatized, childhood anecdote as they strolled, and she soon had them all laughing.

Ivan's laughter rang loudest. He told tales of his own, often of his exploits when they were not present.

Bragging still! Would he never outgrow this? He was a year younger than her and Sareen, but what did a year matter now? Ten years younger than Layton, but Ivan cared nothing for him. Her mother used to say that the youngest were often jealous—to pay it no heed, and he would stop. Indeed, 'twas easier to ignore than to challenge his stories, for he was prone to petty rages. Beth doubted he would ever outgrow his braggart tendencies. Which shouldn't be her concern, but their names were coupled. A shiver coursed through her.

"Are you chilled," Layton asked.

"Nay."

He probably knew something was wrong—Layton noticed things—but he didn't inquire. Instead, he mentioned one of their pretend hunts from years ago and got the conversation back on track. Her smile flickered. Had his years of diffusing squabbles aided him in achieving his diplomatic position?

He had always been the practical one. Older, certain, but even now, his doublet was of sober hue, unlike Ivan's flashy garb. Odd that the practical one had the most exciting life.

How she envied him! Not the onerous task of contending with foreigners. No one could envy that! But he got to travel through all the duchies of Lavaycia. She was lucky to get to Selta Castle twice a year to visit Sareen. Here, a little more often, but that was not pure pleasure. The other four duchies, she rarely saw. And north—never.

Her gaze reached toward that forbidden compass point, but the groomed woods were all her eyes could grasp. Would she ever see the tower trees she'd heard tell of? Or the treacherous River Thane on the northern border of Lavaycia? Faint chance. Her father wouldn't even take her to see the majestic falls of the River Vale. And *that* was just a couple hours' ride.

A cry startled Beth.

Sareen gasped. "Is that a babe?" She rose on tiptoe, anxious eyes searching the wood.

"More likely a rabbit," Layton said.

Ivan's eyes blazed. Beth hated that strange smile of his. Lips stretched, revealing his teeth, and turning downward at the corners. Even more, she hated the excitement that always accompanied it.

"A rabbit, certain," Ivan declared, "and I know where. Come."

He grabbed her hand and dragged her with him, his grip so tight, Beth feared her bones would snap. At least Layton kept pace, and Sareen tagged along behind.

Then she saw it.

Beth jerked her hand from Ivan's, only possible because he had forgotten her.

Sareen shrieked in her ear.

The poor rabbit! Its leg caught in an iron trap. Tormented and crying still.

"Ah!" Ivan exhaled his words with relish. "Perfect!" He circled the terrified little creature.

"Why must you trap rabbits?" Layton demanded. "Can you not handle a bow?"

"I can. Better than you, I would wager. But arrows spoil the pelt."

The rabbit's pitiful cry sent quivers through Beth's nerves.

Layton drew his dagger. "If you will not put it out of its misery, I shall."

"Put away your blade." Ivan's voice dripped scorn as he dropped to one knee. He grabbed the rabbit's head and shoulders, then twisted sharply. "There, you see. Not a mark on it, save that little foot, which we don't need anyway." He opened the trap and reset it, gathering up leaves and sprinkling them upon it.

Sareen drew her flounced skirt close and uttered a frightened squeak. "Where else do you have traps?"

"Fear not, little Sareen. Shall I not lead you safely from the woods?" He stood, the dead rabbit dangling from his right hand, and offered his other arm to Beth. "And you, my fair lady."

"Nay!" She clutched Layton's arm, which he promptly bent for her. "You are cruel! I will not walk with you."

"So squeamish." Ivan's tone mocked. "Do you not know where your meat comes from? Will you revile me because I prefer a bloodless kill?"

"Nay, 'tis your perverse enjoyment that revolts me!"

His head jerked back, nostrils flaring. Ere his rage burst forth, he seemed to recollect. His heavy breath quieted. "Favor whom you will. I hope he can lead you safely past the traps. If so, don't fear I will hold offense when we sit at dinner tonight. Be assured that I will share this morsel with you." He lifted his kill like a trophy. "Now, pray excuse me. I must get this to the chef." He set off at a run through the trees.

Sareen uttered a little gasp, and Layton breathed a soft *sh*.

Nausea turned Beth's stomach. She would *not* eat that!

When Ivan was beyond their voices, Sareen squeaked, "How will we find our way out?"

"Fear nothing," Layton said. "We need only retrace our steps."

Sareen's glance darted about as though the ground would attack her. "But I don't know where—"

"I do know." Layton took her hand. "All is well."

"But what if—"

"You will follow behind me, your hand on my shoulder. Should I make a mistake, my boots will bear the harm." He turned as he spoke, positioning her. "You will only tread where I have safely walked." He looked down at Beth. "Will you stay at my side or follow?"

He gave no hint that fears may be absurd. Only calm certainty. She released a tight breath. "At your side."

He guided them safely back to the path, and Sareen settled herself enough to take his other arm.

Beth worked the joints of the hand Ivan had nigh crushed. How could a walk in the woods turn so vile? Their *day of remembrance* would never be fondly recalled. A quiver ran through her. Would she remember this day as his wife? Her stomach roiled.

They were not yet espoused. She neared her eighteenth birthday—old enough to wed— but her father had declared he would wait longer to choose her husband. And everyone knew why. Because Ivan—the obvious choice—was a year younger than she.

They walked in silence at first, but Sareen couldn't manage it any longer. "I've never seen anyone kill an animal like that. I ride with my father and brothers on hunts. They never do that. Gloating and chattering while the poor beast suffers!" She leaned forward to look at Beth. "Does your father allow such a thing?"

Revolting thought. "My father has never let me ride with the hunt. I—I cannot answer."

"I've hunted with him," Layton said. "Your father and his men seek a quick kill, as does any gentlemen of Lavaycia."

"Disgusting!" Sareen hissed. "Those traps! Do you realize the one we saw was lucky? I daresay others lie in a trap for hours. Or days!"

Beth looked away. There were whispers...stories that her parents declared must not be spoken. Did they think she would follow blindly? She glowered. Of course, they did. 'Twas her duty.

Sareen broke off her ranting as they passed through the hunting gate in the castle's north wall. Layton guided them into the garden, rather than through it, and found a curved bench.

Sareen was about to sit beside Beth, when her gaze seemed to catch on the second-floor balcony of the mansion. She sighed, "I must go. My mother beckons me." She bestowed an impulsive hug on Beth.

"Thank you for walking with me, my dear," Beth murmured into her curls.

As Sareen returned to the mansion, Layton sat on the opposite end of the bench, leaving appropriate distance between him and Beth. He never took advantage of any opportunities to draw near. He was too far removed in rank, and she never thought of him that way. He was the big cousin who had lifted her out of a bush, set her back on her pony, and untangled the sticks from her dusky curls.

"Layton..." She licked her lips. "What do you think of...of the way Ivan killed the rabbit. *Truly* think of it?"

He took a moment to answer. "'Tis not so much a matter of whether it died by a broken neck or a dagger. The poorest folk of Lavaycia snare rabbits. 'Tis the only way they can get meat. But that—obviously—does not explain Ivan's behavior. Truly...it is disturbing."

"If we were to speak of this," Beth said, "he would have plenty of excuses for the actual deed. His manner is hard to describe without sounding like..." Her breath hissed between set teeth. "Like a hysterical woman. You cannot imagine how I hate those words!"

"Then 'tis well they do not apply to you. I have seen you in difficulties, Beth, and seen you angry, but never hysterical."

"Thank you!" Her quick smile faded. "Ivan's father would call me hysterical in an instant." She fidgeted. "In fairness, though, his wife gives him many such displays." She bit her lip, remembering the whispers that had followed a particularly awful screaming fit.

She shook her head. "Layton, I fear to wed Ivan, and I fear to say *why* I would refuse him." Ah, that was it. She raised her brows. "There, I have my answer, do I not? I must stop wavering between the two and decide. 'Tis not such a hard decision, after all. My dread of wedding him is far greater than my fear of the battle."

Layton laughed. "And don't I know the determination you can hide beneath ladylike airs."

She straightened her posture. "Thus, I make my stand. I will not wed Ivan Maerton."

"Hm. And now, the diplomat in me must speak. Be wise in how you state that and to whom."

CHAPTER 5

Beyond the Border Lands

T ristan couldn't tear his eyes from the castle. Though half obscured by trees, it held him spellbound. James and Cotrell lingered on either side of him, taking in the sight from this hilltop perch.

Twin towers rose from the largest structure within. More towers jutted from the curtain wall. It glowed a dusky white in the sunshine, a contrasting backdrop to stark limbs and branches fringed with gold and burgundy. Dauntless fidgeted under him, as though he too thrilled at the sight of the castle.

Cotrell's gray tossed its head and neighed. "'Twould seem that our horses are thinking of a stable."

"After last night," James said, "*I* would sleep in a stable!"

For Tristan, no words were adequate. He started down the hill. More nut trees joined the woods. Soon, their thick trunks marched in rows up a rising slope.

James pointed to the right. "Over there. The shorter trees."

Tristan turned to parallel him down a row of gnarled, bare trunks with younger offspring scattered between.

"Fruit trees," James said. "This was an orchard. A pity the fruit has fallen."

Cotrell drew near a branch and stood in his stirrups to reach a forlorn apple overhead. "Perhaps there is one left for you," he said, plucking it and handing it to James.

He inspected it and took a bite. "Mm. Tart, but not overmuch. Would you like a taste, my lord?"

"Nay. You deserve far more than an apple for following my escapades."

James smiled on him and nodded toward the western border of the orchard. "Those bushes gone wild there—they may bear fruit in summer." His teeth crunched into the apple again.

"There is nothing beyond them," Cotrell said. "They must edge the cliff."

"Aye," Tristan murmured. The bushes formed a long border, reaching all the way to the castle's northwest tower. A small gate was set in the north wall, perhaps useful at harvest time. By design, 'twas clear it could only be opened from within.

He raised his eyes to study the battlement atop the wall. The crenellation gaps were empty, but if a skilled archer hid behind a merlon—be that ever so unlikely—they would be within range. He twitched the reins. "Come up." Dauntless lifted his head from the apple-strewn ground, and Tristan led them through the woods surrounding the castle.

The curtain wall formed an irregular pentagon, built from a fair stone that reminded him of Verenlia's edifices.

"These woods are too close," Cotrell said.

"Aye." Tristan gestured as they progressed. "The nearest trees have the thinnest trunks. This area would have been cleared. Fields, perhaps, but the forest has encroached."

They found an open stretch with a few cobblestones peeking through the dirt. To their left, the road must have headed northeasterly, and to the right, it curved around to the primary gate, set in the south wall. Another overgrown road ran south, swallowed up by the forest.

From that road, Tristan stared up at the regal towers that flanked the gatehouse. The sun's rays set the castle alight, its beauty undimmed by time. Beyond the curtain wall, the inner towers bore a row of windows beneath their blue peaked roofs. No colors flew from any of the tower masts.

A strange thrill suffused him, making it hard to hear Cotrell.

"There is no sign of man or horse upon the ground, nor anything bigger than a fox. Odd, but welcome."

"At the moment," James said, "'tis the gate that troubles me. We will find no safety here if it remains closed."

"True." Tristan studied the gate. Drawbridge style, though there was no moat.

Cotrell scanned the walls. "It seems utterly deserted, but shall I shout?"

"Aye."

Cotrell tilted his head back and took a deep breath. "Hail, keeper of the gate!"

A hawk sailed from a tower, and a flock of pigeons vacated the walls. If anything, the castle seemed more deserted.

"If birds roost, no one walks the walls," Tristan said. "We'll need a likely tree."

They dismounted and left the horses with James. Cotrell began searching to his right, while Tristan turned leftward. He found the perfect specimen near the southwest tower. Tall enough and damaged, it leaned already toward the castle wall. "Over here," he called out.

Cotrell joined him, and together they tried to turn that lean to their advantage. The tree proved stubborn. Since they had no ax, they tried to pull it with a rope and horses. It creaked, but they couldn't get enough leverage. Cotrell tried his throwing line, hoping to anchor it higher, but the branches broke away.

Tristan glared up at the tree. "What I wouldn't give for a chat with Captain D'Jorge right now." That man could figure out the most perplexing dilemmas. "What would he do?"

They stared at the bare trunk and spoke in unison. "Climb it."

Tristan smiled and said, "Give me the end of your line."

The iron weight allowed him to loop a firm knot that could be easily tied and loosened. Tristan pulled it tight as far up the trunk as he could, then gripped it to climb.

"I can go up, my lord."

"Nay, not an old man like you."

"I'm thirty-nine!" Cotrell snarled.

Tristan grinned and handed his bow and sword belt to Cotrell, for they were already in the way. He dug the heels of his boots in and began his ascent. A slow business, what with moving the line and the crumbling bark that fell from the trunk. As the lean increased, he needed the line less for leverage. Cotrell had tied another rope to the dangling end. Not much farther up the narrowing trunk and Tristan should be able to attach the line where it couldn't slip.

To the east, a wolf let out a long howl. That didn't necessarily mean much, but still...an ominous reminder. This was all taking much longer than it should have.

Below him, James held all three horses near the gate.

Cotrell called up to him. "Do not rush and grow careless."

Chest against the tree, Tristan bent his legs and scooted higher. He knocked off loose bark and scooted another foot. Something snapped at the base of the tree. A long, ominous crack vibrated up the trunk.

"Hold on!" Cotrell shouted.

Tristan clung, wrapping arms and legs around the trunk and pressing the side of his head tight against the wood.

The treetop struck the wall and bounced, nearly flinging Tristan off.

His muscles shrieked, but he managed to cling as the tree

settled against the battlements. Oh, was he going to hurt tomorrow!

Debris rained to the ground as Cotrell shouted, "Are you all right?"

He managed a weak laugh. "Aye. Whose stupid idea was this?"

Cotrell's voice shook. "We'll blame D'Jorge."

Another wolf howled.

"If we can stay alive long enough to tell him," Tristan muttered. He scooted forward, despite complaints from his ribs. Not much farther, and he crawled off onto a flat-topped merlon. He jumped down to the walkway and ran toward the gatehouse, his shadow long before him. What were the wolves doing?

He shoved the tower's wooden door, which groaned open. Stone steps curved down one wall and up the other. He crossed the wooden floor and flung the next door open.

Two great wheels with turning pegs...chains with counterweights raised high... He peered through a slot in the floor on the bailey side. Iron. It must be a portcullis. On the opposite side, there was not enough light to see, but it must be the same. Where was the mechanism to lower the draw gate? He groped in the dim space between the portcullis wheel and the exterior wall of the gatehouse. His hands closed on another wheel.

He tried turning it one way, then the other, but it only clanked as he shoved. He followed the sound and found a chain. Groping its length, he discovered a bar shoved through the heavy links, pinning it. Wolves in mind, Tristan jerked the bar out and tried the wheel again. This time, it turned, groaning. Around and around. A bit of light filtered up through the floor gaps.

"James. Cotrell," Tristan yelled, "are you near the gate?

"Aye, but we're clear," Cotrell answered. "Keep lowering."

Tristan turned it as fast as he could. A counterweight rose through a gap.

Cotrell finally called out. "'Tis down. Raise the portcullis."

His voice sounded urgent. Why? Had he spotted wolves? Or worse?

Tristan hurried back between the other two wheels. He found the pin at once, jerked it free, then dropped his weight against the turning pegs. This wheel moved freer. He heard Cotrell say, "Get under." Was that the snap of a bow? The counterweight was out of sight now. Tristan heard the horses clop onto stone beneath him. And another bowstring snap.

"Drop the portcullis," Cotrell shouted.

Growls, a snap, and a yelp.

Tristan ran to the opposite side and threw his weight into it again, until the wheel stopped with a final clank. Why did that bow keep snapping? "Are you safe?" he shouted.

"Aye." Cotrell's answer sounded lazy. "Safe, if you can call it that on the smelly end of three horses. Anytime you want to open the other portcullis would be fine with me."

Relief drew a breathy laugh from Tristan. He replaced the bar, pinning the outer portcullis, released the inner one, and raised it. "You are working these wheels next time," he called down.

"You're the one who wanted to climb that tree."

Tristan groped his way down the dim tower, feeling almost giddy.

James met him at the bottom and looked him up and down. "You made it in one piece?"

"Aye, albeit a battered piece." Tristan rubbed the tender side of his head. "We are not traveling tomorrow."

The horses fanned out beyond the gate, though not far. They eyed the bailey, ears twitching this way and that. Cotrell was intent on something just under the archway, then a flame sprang to life.

"Ah, well-found," Tristan said, as Cotrell placed a torch in a bracket beside the arch, then lit another for the opposite side.

Golden sunset faded into darkening blue above, and shadows stretched across the bailey. They would soon need more light.

Cotrell scanned the expanse. "You scouted this all out before you opened the gate, right?"

"That's your task." The mansion—for that was no keep—dominated Tristan's vision. It stretched along the western wall, much broader than its four-storied height. 'Twas built from pale stone, a fair setting for its broad, glazed windows. A decorative battlement with wide crenellations lined its flat roof. The twin, peaked towers rose from within that stately border.

The horses headed for the faded greenery of a terrace, which encircled a courtyard before the mansion's arched entrance. Broad steps descended the terrace to the solid rock bailey. Simpler buildings with one or two stories clustered along the eastern and northern walls.

Cotrell pointed toward a long building with two wide doors and smaller split-doors. "The stable—and that looks like a well in front of it."

There was little that mattered more than water. They strode to the circular stone wall with a trough extending from it. Cotrell found a pebble and threw it into the well. When it splashed, the three of them shared a smile.

A bare windlass perched above the well. "We need a bucket and line," Tristan said. "Let's try the stable."

James found a lantern by the door. Striking the flint, he commented, "Again we find lighting paraphernalia made ready at an entrance."

By the glow of a few lanterns, they discovered rope and a resin-coated bucket. Cotrell began hoisting water from the well. The sound of it splashing down the trough drew the thirsty horses.

"I suggest we eat," James said, "before exploring furth—"

A distant yowl brought them erect.

"'Tis a long way off." Cotrell dumped another bucket of water and said, "My stomach agrees with you, James."

Tristan nodded. "Let's just make sure we can keep enough lanterns burning to—"

Another yowl. *Much* closer.

A fiery chill coursed through Tristan. "The tree!" He raced for the gate, footsteps pounding behind him. Grabbing a lit torch, he ran for the tower stairs. Firelight flickered over stone walls and armaments stacked along them. He grabbed a spear and dashed up the winding steps.

At the top of the wall, he sprinted for the tree. His worst fear materialized. The top-most branches bounced. Something was on the trunk.

He caught a glimpse of it through a crenellation. Tawny and black—a big cat, but not a monster. They had a chance.

"Help me push the tree off!" he shouted to Cotrell, close on his heels.

He ducked under a branch and climbed atop a merlon on the far side. The trunk rested against the gap of a narrow crenellation. Cotrell pushed from below, while Tristan tried to pry with the butt end of the spear. The trunk moved, but not enough. He couldn't risk breaking the spear.

The cat's hind leg slipped as the trunk shifted. It snarled and kept climbing.

"It won't work," Cotrell shouted. He darted back to another crenellation, pulling his bow from his shoulder. His arrows flew, but they only annoyed the cat, catching in its hide but not penetrating.

Tristan pulled the spear free and tested its balance. Longer than the cat's legs—might work once the beast was in range. He snatched up the torch and waved it, flinging a few sparks toward the cat. It snarled and crept nearer.

More running feet, and James flung an armload of arrows before Cotrell. "What else do you need?"

"Give me Cotrell's torch," Tristan shouted, pointing at it across the tree. He grabbed it from James. "Bring more of them."

James sprinted away.

Tristan waved both torches, to no avail. He dropped to one knee and shoved a torch under the trunk, along with a broken branch. Keeping the other torch nearby, he hefted the spear. A poor weapon for a man perched on a merlon. A forward lunge would be his death. He braced himself, hooking his foot against the merlon's edge.

Cotrell continued to shoot. An arrow tore through the cat's ear. He must be aiming for the eyes. A small moving target. Still, the beast came.

Tristan jabbed with the spear. It pierced the hide but glanced off bone. He tried again. The enraged cat swatted it away with such power, the spear tore from Tristan's grip. It spun through the air and clattered to the bailey below.

Running footsteps hammered nearer.

Tristan grabbed his torch and brandished it again. Once that cat got over, they were all dead. If the beast didn't fear fire, he would ram the torch into its gaping jaws. Claws would rake him, but the others might survive.

James reached them. A small fire flickered among the branches. James shoved another torch into it and held a bucket up to Tristan, shouting, "Oil. Douse the trunk."

With the cat's claws not six feet away, Tristan flung oil along the trunk and down toward the beast. Flames licked up from below. Tristan vaulted away from the sudden blaze, landing beside the next crenellation.

The cat twisted and lunged sideways, sending another loud crack through the trunk. The creature hit the ground with a yowl and a few sparks. It fled westward, its tawny shape disappearing down the dark, wooded slope.

Tristan panted. A pity the cat hadn't truly caught fire. He joined the others. They worked the torches like pokers, breaking branches to feed the fire. Flames licked around the stub of the trunk.

They paused when yowls sounded from the slope where the cat had fled. Two beasts, and then just one. Something heavy was dragged down the steep hill westward.

"I hope the loser was our visitor," Cotrell said.

The burning trunk shifted under its own weight, and with a final crack, collapsed beyond the wall.

Cotrell leaned into a crenellation to peer down. "No flames." He straightened. "The burnt end is wedged up against the wall, but I suppose we should pitch some water over."

They chewed dry meat while drawing water, carrying, and dumping it over the moonlit wall. Until the windlass handle snapped off in Tristan's grip. The full bucket descended with a splash. He sighed. Were his hands not raw enough already? He grabbed the rope and pulled the bucket up.

James returned with an empty bucket and tipped the water into it. Unperturbed as ever, he said, "'Tis enough. I will tell Cotrell."

When at last they had stabled the horses, Tristan carried a lantern into the stable-hands' room at the far end. Cots between partitions on one side, table and benches on the other. Even a basin and water cans on a sideboard. He hung the lantern from a chain that dangled overhead and sat down facing the cots. "James, your wish to sleep in a stable is fulfilled."

"This is palatial after the last few nights," Cotrell said. He took a blanket from a set of shelves and shook it out. "Why isn't this moth-eaten?"

"Cedar," James said, pulling Tristan's boots off.

"In a stable?" Cotrell's dirty face skewed.

"Not all of it, but in here and the external walls, aye." James looked up at Tristan. "Your hair is singed, my lord. Are you burned?"

"Nay." He forced a tired smile. "What do I look like?"

Cotrell smirked. "Sooty. I think I'll carry one last bucket of water."

Too exhausted to wash more than hands and face in the cool well water, Tristan soon stretched out on a cot. One of the others extinguished the lantern.

The questions resurfaced, weaving through his tired mind. Who had built this grand castle? Why did they never return?

CHAPTER 6

Within the Castle

Tristan was last awake the next morn. He groaned as he sat up. Best to move and try to work some of this out. Besides...something smelled good.

He found Cotrell tending a fire and... "What are those?"

"Pigeons."

Tristan's stomach rumbled. "You, my friend, are without peer!"

Cotrell chuckled.

Tristan and James carried benches outside, and they consumed their feast around the fire, relishing every scrap of fresh meat. Across the bailey, the mansion fairly glowed in the rising sun, beckoning.

James tilted his head toward the mansion and asked, "Is that where you'll start your exploring?"

Trust James to guess his longing. "I'd like to, but it must wait. We should walk the walls first."

Cotrell nodded and tore off another bite of meat.

"Do you not believe we're safe within the castle?" James asked.

Did he? "Probably. What think you, Cotrell? Could the enormous black beast that took our mare jump the walls?"

Cotrell chewed, frowning. "That depends. How similar was it to the tawny cat we fought last night?"

"*Much* bigger. You must know that. The shape of its head and snout were similar...as far as I could tell by firelight. All black, too, but that means nothing, especially since the tawny one had black markings. Why do you ask?"

Cotrell stared at the fire. "Tawny was a poor jumper—for a cat, that is—and a poor climber too. I thought sure it would be up that tree in seconds, but..." He shook his head. "Its hind quarters didn't seem right, somehow."

"Injured?"

"Nay...ungainly. Like the back legs didn't work well with the front legs. Reminds me of what you said about the black's teeth. Tawny reeked like the black too." His words slowed. "'Tis oddly named. I could see calling it a fox-cat, since it has that long snout. But why vixicat?"

Unanswerable, but James suggested a possibility. "'Tis said that a vixen with kits is the most vicious of animals."

"Mm. Unfair," Cotrell murmured. "But to your question, my lord, if the black is just a bigger specimen, I doubt it can jump high. Its weight will work against it too. These walls are *tall*."

"Agreed—and built by those who would've known of the beasts. Let's walk the full circuit to get the overall view. Then the mansion."

They started by the gatehouse. From the circular tower, Tristan looked through a narrow window at the exterior wall. A blackened streak marred it, though he saw no actual damage.

They climbed to the top. Gazing down from the height, Cotrell said, "The wolf I killed while you were working the gates —'tis gone. Entirely."

"Hm." A small scavenger would take a piece and run with it,

but the whole carcass... "Only a vixicat is big enough to drag away these overgrown wolves. But why?" Tristan mused. "Why would they bother?" He considered the woods descending the steep westward slope. Dense, like they had never been cleared.

They continued around. On the western side, the fourth floor of the mansion backed the curtain wall. They found no entrance at this level and continued past it. The view was stunning—a deep valley stretching to the sea—but Tristan kept walking.

James found much to comment on, from the fine details of the castle's design to the provisions stored in the towers.

The north to eastern walls revealed the extent of the common buildings. There were more than Tristan had first assumed. Broad spaces, as well. The horses rested in the one behind the stable.

Tristan paused to look closer at another expanse. "A training yard, I believe."

"Aye," Cotrell replied, nodding to the long building opposite. "That could be barracks."

James pointed to a smaller building. "A shame that one has a tree growing from the roof. 'Tis likely ruined, but all in all, the structures look sound. Better than I would have expected. Cedar is a durable wood."

Tristan held back an affectionate chuckle.

Cotrell grinned. "We no sooner stepped within walls, ere the steward inside you began to speak."

"Nay, before," Tristan said. "'Twas among the nut trees."

James let his prim smile be seen. "What else would you have, my lord?"

Tristan clapped him on the shoulder as they turned to walk again. "I could ask for nothing more. You are all things as the need arises."

They descended the tower on the east side of the gatehouse, marveling again at how well-stocked everything was. A pipe and tobacco tin in the gatekeeper's quarters, arrows in every tower, lanterns and jugs of oil at primary entrances, and much more. The provisions of an occupied castle.

"One thing is certain," Tristan said, exiting the final tower. "The staff of this castle intended to return." His pulse quickened as he strode across the baily. "And now, for the mansion!"

Tristan ran up the steps of the courtyard—an elongated half-moon, paved with broad stones. The central area was open, and on either side, pathways spoked between weedy beds. Benches stood at regular intervals. James walked aside to inspect a statue, but Tristan strode on toward the marble archway, where two carved, wooden doors beckoned him. A door somewhere must yield access. Please, let it be these.

He grasped the gilded handles, cool within his grip. The doors shifted at his tug but didn't open.

"Locked from within?" Cotrell suggested.

"Perhaps, but not barred." He felt something odd within the scrollwork of the handles. Something that moved. Latches? He worked them until iron scraped. His pulse quickened again, and he stepped back, pulling the doors wide.

In one second, sunlight evicted decades of darkness.

The men stood spellbound. Tristan took a few steps forward, his boots sending soft echoes through the hall. A sound not heard in many a long year. He had a strange fancy that the mansion expelled emptiness through the wide-open doors.

White marble lined the floor and walls. Black marble framed a large fireplace and formed the balustrades of two curved staircases and a gallery above. Paintings in gilded frames, gold sconces between them, even the shadowed ceiling, twenty feet above, seemed to be decorated with relief carving. Out of harmony with all this grandeur, drab sheeting covered the furniture.

James lifted the nearest cloth and revealed a chair upholstered with satiny indigo.

Cotrell turned back beside the doors. "What a surprise. Oil

lamps await us." He rapped a striker and soon had three hand-lamps lit.

Archways at the sides of the hall led to other rooms. The men wandered through the right archway first and found a salon. To the left was a library. Two smaller arches on either side of the fireplace connected to an extension of the hall, which stretched to the back of the mansion.

James pulled aside heavy draperies, and light spilled in. "We must be beneath the wall walkway." He twisted a latch, and the casements swung inward, allowing the western breeze to waft through. After a moment, James turned from the view to Tristan. "You say little, my lord."

"I am too awed and puzzled," Tristan replied. "Had I built this, I would never cease caring for it until I passed it to my heirs. And if not to heirs, to *someone*." He shook his head, turning in a slow circle. "I could not bear to think of it unappreciated. Discarded. Who would do such a thing?"

Tristan shook off the mood. "There is much here to be seen. Let us divide and look quickly through the rooms, meeting at the center again as we complete each floor. In particular, I want to find access to the towers."

This they did. James found the kitchens and cellars, which pleased him, but it was Cotrell who found the curved wall and door of the south tower.

Tristan could hardly keep from running ahead as Cotrell led the way to his find.

In the cool darkness of the tower base, Tristan felt like he was at the bottom of a well. A spiral staircase ascended through the center of a partial ceiling above him. Their lamps revealed a door at each floor, but they did not pause to look beyond. On the sixth level, windows pierced the walls. A writing desk and shelves filled with ledger books lent an official air to the room.

James gazed longingly at the ledgers, as the other two extinguished their lamps. He sighed as he set his lamp with theirs, then followed them higher.

Tristan moved away from the top step into a room encircled by windows. "Now *this* is a view worth the climb."

The sparkling sea—so vast Tristan's mind could not grasp it—stretched across the western reaches. The valley, descending below him, was still cloaked in leaves and contrasted yellow, orange, and red against the distant blue. North, he could make out the highest peak of the ridge, though most of it was hidden behind the hills. They looked like mounds from above, continuing one after another, as he walked around to the east. South lay the plain they had originally sought. 'Twas a swath of grassland so long, he could not glimpse the eastern end. The more he saw, the less he understood.

Beside him, Cotrell said, "If we had followed the plain, we would have found the castle."

"Aye," Tristan murmured, frowning. "Which raises even more questions."

"What is this?" James asked, touching a brass tube mounted on a three-legged stand.

Tristan ran his fingers along the polished surface and pulled the leather cover off the end. Curved glass within. "Ah!" He stretched the word. "I hope it's what I think it is." Uncovering the narrow end, he bent to look through it. The forest across the plain jumped near. He laughed deep in his throat. He'd heard of such devices in Verenlia, but never seen one.

"Look through it, James." He laughed again as James startled backwards from the view. "'Tis called a distance glass," Tristan said.

Cotrell's eyes glowed. "I've *always* wanted a glimpse through one of those."

Tristan gestured for him to take a look. "Treat it gently. I believe the internal alignment is critical."

Cotrell found no words at first, but his face revealed wonder and churning ideas. A moment later, he figured out how to work the swivel mount and began turning it to sweep the vista. Alternating between normal view and the glass, he said, "Do you realize how much this will help with mapping?" He seemed to recollect himself and stepped away with a nod. "Pardon, my lord. You must wish to see it too."

Tristan's shoulders shook. "I'll try to keep it short." He turned the glass through a full circle, even though the north view wasn't good without moving the stand. 'Twould be torment to keep it from Cotrell, so he stepped aside rather than moving it.

James meandered around the space, trying to stay out of the way of the swiveling glass. He found the sliding bolts to release the windows. "These could use a good cleaning."

The corners of Cotrell's eyes creased. "Open is quite good enough for now. Thank you." He bent to the glass again.

James's prim smile snuck out. "I gather you will be here for some time. If you'll excuse me, I'll just see what those ledgers contain. Don't forget to close the windows before you descend."

Tristan nodded and began to circle the room as James left. Even without the distance glass, the view was amazing. Not just the beauty of it—discerning the lay of the land was far more critical. He studied it, pondering. "We are much closer to the plain than the ridge."

"Aye," Cotrell murmured. "We took the long way around. The plain must be what Burk called the low route. Eastward, it dips between the two forests, probably muddy in spring." He swung the glass along the far forest, then paused, his mouth agape. He straightened and stared at the seaward end of that distant woodland. "Those trees are incredible!"

"Indeed. I've ne'er seen nor heard of such." Tristan took a moment to study them through the distance glass again. Vast trunks rose so high he couldn't hazard a guess in feet. Nor could he keep the awe from his voice. "They look to be as big around as this tower." The upper reaches were cloaked, apparently evergreen. Haze lurked between them. That, and the dark forest floor, lent an ominous air. "Intriguing though it is, that forest is the least of our concerns."

He moved away to let Cotrell use the glass again and stared

out to the sea. Though the view enchanted, his thoughts kept prodding the puzzle. "Why all this talk of the castle being hidden? 'Tis *visible* from the plain."

"All I can reckon," Cotrell said, "is that they don't travel westward." He straightened. "When no one at the inn could tell me the distance to the sea, I asked if they knew of anyone who'd been there. They looked at me like I was daft. One of them said, 'What would anyone go down there for?'" Cotrell shrugged. "I suppose the vixicat stories could keep them away. Seems strange though. All this open land, and no one farms it."

"That part could make sense. The land along the River Thane looks fertile, but it is too rocky to plow. They say the grass roots run as deep as tree roots. Trees can be felled and ne'er grow back, but grass always returns."

Cotrell quirked a smile at him. "You're beginning to sound like James."

Tristan uttered a soft laugh. "I may not have a landed inheritance, but I was taught to manage an estate along with my brothers. There's more to it than you would think."

Cotrell tilted his head. "Why have you no land?"

The question caught Tristan off guard, sparking memory of disappointment. "My father intended that I would, though his own holdings could not be split among so many sons. That is why he set aside coin for me. He was still looking for suitable land when he died."

Cotrell viewed only him now. "Why haven't you sought land of your own?"

His father's passing...nay, he couldn't speak of that. Instead, Tristan said, "Youth at first, I suppose. Then a war you may recall, since you fought at my side." He paused, but Cotrell only nodded. "Since then..." Tristan leaned against a windowsill. "Have you noticed a lot of land lying vacant around Moorelin?"

Cotrell's lips twisted down. "I've never paid much attention. I think of land in terms of scouting, not owning. I wouldn't even bother with a cottage if I hadn't married and had children."

His countenance fell a bit when he mentioned marriage, for his wife had died of a fever years earlier. His mother-in-law cared for his son and daughter now. Though Cotrell rarely let it show, in moments like these, Tristan sensed how Cotrell missed them when he followed Tristan abroad. And knew just as well that Cotrell didn't want to dwell on loss.

Tristan replied to his first comment. "There is no vacant land for you to pay attention to. Maybe a few parcels here and there, but certainly not an estate. 'Tis all so...settled."

Cotrell's eyes crinkled at the corners. "You are a strange mix, my lord. You want an estate, yet you want adventure too."

"Now, *you* sound like James!" He closed the nearest casement. "We've much of this castle yet to walk."

They both closed windows and met on the north side. Tristan pointed. "You see how much grayer the distant hills look there. As though there is a wider gap before them that runs westward. Do you suppose it could be the ravine that Burk spoke of?"

"It may be." Cotrell squinted at it a moment longer, and his voice dipped. "I think that's where the black vixicat took the mare."

CHAPTER 7

Within the Castle

Tristan and Cotrell descended the winding stairs and found James as engrossed in ledgers as they had been in the land.

"My lord…" He sounded spellbound. "Someone kept records here each dawn and sunset."

Tristan pretended interest. "Oh?"

"Some are about the weather and such, but they also tracked the activity of the vixicats. Apparently, 'tis not always the same."

That ended pretense. "What differs?"

"I'm not sure yet. They counted the number of fights each night. They seemed to know the size of the cat from its sound. The deeper yowls are from the biggest cats. If they're mismatched in a fight, the biggest usually wins, though not always, and…" He paused. "They call the fights *kills*."

"Strange," Cotrell said. "Animals don't usually kill their own kind, even when fighting for mates or territory."

Tristan looked at the ledgers lying open and those stacked on the shelves. "What time span have you checked?"

"Little, my lord. I just pulled a few at random to get a feel for what kind of records they kept. They mentioned mapping the fights." James gestured around. "Though, there are no maps here."

Cotrell's eyes had widened at the word *mapping*, and now he groaned. "I don't suppose they said *where* these maps are, did they?"

"Of course not," James replied with a taunting smile. "They would all have known."

"We must continue our survey of this mansion," Tristan said.

"Doubtless." Cotrell picked up his lamp and relit it from the one James had left burning "But if anyone finds maps or storage tubes, I want to hear you shouting my name!"

They exited the tower on the second floor and split up again, then reconvened in the gallery after a quick check of each room.

"All that I see reminds me of Verenlia," Tristan said, "but the style is much lighter. Not as gaudy as their current tastes."

"True," James said. "This may have been the mode when it was built or perhaps later. Many rooms have an even simpler style. More bare, wooden furniture, and also more deterioration in the textiles. I suspect that part of the mansion has been redecorated since the castle was first built."

Tristan looked out from the gallery at a crystal chandelier, which hung over the front half of the entry hall. "Multiple generations may have lived here."

"Castles take years to build," Cotrell said. "They may have occupied gradually. I don't suppose any of you found maps?"

"Nay," Tristan said. "Let's look over the third floor."

James headed for the stairs. "Bedrooms, I would suspect."

A central salon lay against the west wall, and beside it...was this a chapel?

Tristan's pause, as he held the double doors wide, must have caught the attention of James and Cotrell, for they came to discover what he stared at. A stained-glass window such as he had never seen.

They walked slowly nearer. A rainbow in dozens of shades, subtly blended, filled the upper half of the window. Beneath it, a broad hill touched a clear prism embedded in the azure sky.

Tristan pointed to it. "In the evening, that must catch the rays of the sun and look much like a sunset over that hill."

"I daresay you are right," James said. "The embedded detail of the landscape exceeds any I've seen in Moorelin. Surely, 'tis a vineyard on the hill and a wheat field below."

"Aye," Tristan murmured.

Windows on either side, each a half-arch, framed the central masterpiece. Though clear, their beveled panes fragmented the view beyond. The sun, still high, cast flecks of color on the narrow table before the window.

"'Tis not a room for looking out," Tristan said. "'Tis a room for receiving light within."

"All in rainbow shades by sunset, I would think," Cotrell said. "Pretty, I suppose, but it seems strange as the primary symbol in a chapel."

Hm. Was there a reason? "'Tis said that the story of the rainbow is in all the varied religions of the lands." Tristan looked down at the altar cloth covering the table. 'Twas a simple rectangle, divided into two triangles from corner to corner—one side snowy white and the other black. At least, it must have been in days past. Now faded to murky gray. "In Moorelin, we say a rainbow represents hope and protection, but Verenlians interpret it as a marker between good and evil. They say the rainbow appeared when evil had almost won, then good resurged to start afresh." He tapped the altar cloth. "The Verenlian symbol of light and dark in an eternal battle, which neither can win."

Cotrell smirked. "The black side seems to have suffered irreparable loss."

"Fitting," Tristan said. "I find their symbolism puzzling. Never have I seen light fail to banish darkness. Indeed, darkness itself is only named when something else blocks the light. Thus, the moon glows to remind us that light is still shining behind us, even when the entire world blocks it."

"Aye," James said. "I do find *hope* to be the more useful interpretation of a rainbow."

Tristan closed his fingers on the faded cloth and swept it from the table, revealing white marble. He handed the cloth to James. "Burn this. Let's take a look at the other rooms."

Mostly bedrooms, a closet full of linens, and a nursery with forlorn toys. One room, in particular, captured Tristan's interest. Clearly, the master's bedroom, adjoined to the mistress's daintier chamber through an elegant sitting room. Tristan strode back to the master's room, remembering what James had said of older styles. As he pushed the faded draperies from the window, an ominous tearing sound made him leave one side half closed. But that was irrelevant compared to what this room might hold. Perhaps some clue to the owner's identity.

Tristan began opening drawers, the wood dark with age. Even clothing had been left. A large trunk held leathers and armor plates. Interesting, but not helpful. The writing desk, perhaps. The drawers beneath it held pens, ink, and paper, but when he lifted the writing surface, he found a book. Simply bound between two leaves of undecorated calfskin. What was this?

He opened the cover. A single word was written on the first page. *Vixicats*. His skin prickled.

Tristan flipped the page, then more, sampling a few and finding the last entry. 'Twas a journal of discoveries. He leaned against the windowsill and began to devour its contents.

There, James found him. "The draperies need replacing, but the mattress feels good."

Tristan startled and blinked at him. "What?"

"Your bed for tonight." James plumped the mattress in a few places. "It may be the only thing in this room that was ever replaced. I went up and checked the fourth floor quickly. Servants' quarters and storage. The floors are creaky, but there is no sign of leaks, which is perhaps the most important thing of all."

A slow smile stretched Tristan's lips as he listened to the prosaic words. "No, James." He held up the journal. "This is the most important thing of all."

Cotrell came to lean against the door frame. "What have you found?"

"A vixicat journal. It references the logs you found, James, but this writer drew conclusions. Things like waxing and waning populations, seasonal behavior changes, and...listen to this!" He flipped to a page he'd marked with one finger and read aloud.

"'The huntsmen have killed two small specimens and recovered the bodies. Thus, we've confirmed sightings of odd distortions. Both had scattered teeth with mixed traits of felines and canines. One had disproportionate hind limbs. The other had a bushy tail and coarse fur. Upon opening the carcasses, we were stunned by greater deformities. Excessive cartilage could explain why arrows rarely penetrate. Perhaps it causes them pain and fuels their viciousness. More surprising, the specimens were both male and female! Our physician dissected them. Though one had a shriveled womb, the other had all internal organs of both sexes. They appeared viable, though unused in this immature vixicat. Whether they can breed with themselves is uncertain. The physician considers it possible, for one testis was turned inward against the birth canal.'"

He looked up from the journal to their wide eyes.

"Wh—" Cotrell swallowed. "What weird force could have been at work to bring about a cross between canine and feline? Nature does not allow it!"

"Indeed," Tristan said. "Likewise, no cat or dog of any sort can reach the size of that black vixicat."

"No wonder the townsfolk dread them," James said. "They seem like demon spawn. This could explain why the castle is forsaken."

Tristan frowned. Did it? He stared at the book in his hand.

"The last entries were not of a man considering surrender. He believed he was nearing the chance to eradicate the beasts entirely."

"How?" Cotrell demanded.

Tristan uttered a wry laugh. "I haven't read the whole thing yet. But this, you'll like. He mentioned going *down* to plot vixicat positions on the map. Down from the tower, I gather. Did you walk the whole south end of the ground floor?"

"Nay!" Cotrell turned from the door, striding for the stairs. "I went no farther than the tower entrance."

In moments, all three of them traversed the interior stone corridor. Their footsteps echoed as they skirted the tower's base. Beyond, lay a heavy wooden door with an iron latch.

Tingling with anticipation, like he was stepping into some ancient mystery, Tristan lifted the latch and pushed the door open. They entered, raising their lamps high.

No luxury here. Massive stone blocks formed the walls, one curving with the tower. Iron candlestands lined two walls. A heavy, rectangular table dominated the center of the room. And on that table...Tristan stepped nearer. Maps.

Cotrell raised his lamp over them.

"Nay, let no spark fall. This parchment is old." Tristan pointed to the candles. "Light them."

This they soon accomplished. While Tristan and Cotrell bent over the maps on the table, James opened a cedar chest. "There are map tubes here, my lord, inscribed with letters and numbers."

Already intent, Tristan murmured, "These two will do for a start." Though the maps were the same size, one covered a broader area. Tristan pointed as he spoke, "Here is the River Thane. Moorelin gets a tiny mention on the edge there, and here is western Verenlia. We must have come through some of these towns."

Two lines were marked leading west from Verenlia, both converging on a pentagon not far from the Great Sea. To the south, an empty area was labeled only with the scrawled name of *Lavaycia*.

Cotrell pointed at it and asked, "What know you of Lavaycia?"

"Not much more than whoever drew this map. Verenlians complain of them."

"Why?"

"Lavaycia has a seaport but allows no merchants to cross their lands. All of Verenlia's trade must pass overland from much farther away, which drives prices up. Some things, they cannot get at all." Tristan pointed again. "No matter to us, for Lavaycia lies south of this forest. Tower Woods, according to the map. A fitting name for those enormous trees we saw. Here's the dividing plain."

"What do they call this forest?" Cotrell leaned in to read, then his voice dripped disdain. "The Wilde?"

"Come now," Tristan soothed. "It has an e on the end. That lends an elegant touch."

"Pha! 'Tis old spelling. They built a castle here and couldn't think of a better name than *The Wilde*?"

Tristan chuckled. "This, from the man who named his horse Grey."

"At least Grey *is* a name," Cotrell grumbled. "And that is Sir Grey, to you."

Tristan gave him a mock bow. "Pray pardon me."

James angled his head, considering the map. "Lavaycians are much nearer neighbors than Verenlians. Yet they haven't come here either."

Tristan shrugged off that oddity. "They are isolationists, reputed to never leave their own borders." He pulled the other map nearer. "What have we here?"

"Local area," Cotrell said, after a quick glance. "They must have drawn this from the tower's vantage point. These hills look accurate. Here's the deeper part between the castle and ridge. 'Tis named—"

They both inhaled at the same moment. Tristan intoned, "Vixicat Lair." He stared at it a moment longer. "That valley we camped in...it leads to the vixicats' lair."

The men exchanged glances.

"When we leave here," Cotrell said slowly, "we are taking a different route."

"That, we are. I'd like to set out soon after sunrise and get over the ridge before noon. It should be possible if we can determine a route from this."

They bent over the map again. Cotrell traced features. "There are two northeast-bound roads marked, and here is the bridge that once crossed the stream. They called that Cave Rapids. Ah, it must flow from this cave marked here. The other road goes around it and then backtracks up to the ridge crossing." He straightened. "Even the long way around, I think we can make it. We can break our fast within the walls and need not stop in the woods."

"Have you forgotten the wolves?" James asked.

"Never," Cotrell replied. "They were at rest. I believe we rode right in among their dens. We will not do so again."

"The extra horse will not slow us either," Tristan said. "'Twas useful among towns, but it made us vulnerable in the woods."

"Remember," Cotrell added, "that we need not take down the entire pack. Only one or two. They don't like prey that fights back." He looked to Tristan. "I'd like to take this up to the tower, maybe to the north one, and study it further."

"Do you plan to leave tomorrow morning?" James asked Tristan.

"I think not." He hesitated a moment, then said, "We must consider provisions, and there is more here that I wish to see. Besides, I would leave all as carefully sealed as we found it...and that means we must find the hidden way out."

James regarded him a moment. "Which would also be the hidden way...in."

Tristan mimicked surprise. "I suppose it would be."

CHAPTER 8

Lavaycia

Beth's maid draped a lace-embellished shawl over her shoulders. Beth tried varied ways of arranging it before the dressing table's mirror. Better to dally in this bedchamber than to spend one more minute than necessary in the salon. Ivan would hover, and it was bad enough that she must sit beside him again at dinner. At least rabbit had not been served last night. Had the chef balked at serving peasants' food, or was there still a chance she'd be subjected to such a course?

She studied the effect of the dainty, curled feather tucked within the high twists of her hair. Dyed to match her amber gown, of course. The maid had styled her dusky locks well. No excuse for delay there.

A firm knock struck the bedroom door.

Odd. She nodded to the maid, who went to answer the knock.

Beth's father entered. A fine doublet was molded to his broad shoulders, and the slashed sleeves revealed his full white shirt.

She rose from the dressing table and met his dark blue eyes, trying to judge his mood. They seemed especially intense tonight. Was it because they reflected his sapphire doublet, or something more?

Regardless, she had yet to find an opportunity to tell him what she must. To describe Ivan's brutality while sounding calm and mature. Probably futile, since her parents only heard her as a child.

Her father motioned for the maid to leave and waited for the door to close before speaking. "Apparently, I should have found time to talk with you earlier."

Her belly fluttered. "What mean you, Father?"

"Think not that I have ever been blind to the noble children. I note your delay in coming down. Your stiffness at dinner last eve and Sareen's daggered glares at Ivan. Which have now turned to daggered words. Tell me what happened."

At least this granted a smooth entrance to the subject. Beth related the bare facts, then adjusted her shawl. "Perhaps it doesn't matter how he killed the poor creature—though I found it *gruesome*—but his pleasure in the deed was...dreadfully disturbing."

Her father's lips remained a hard line.

Had she used too much emphasis? Hating the need to claim support, she said, "Sir Layton was present, if you would like a man's view of the matter."

Her father shook his head. "Now that I know, not a word of this need be repeated."

Heat soared up Beth's back. "More whispers to hide away?" She saw her father's clenching jaw but ignored the warning. "Do you think I do not notice all the hushes? Think no more that I am a child, for indeed I am a woman now. Should I be left ignorant while others choose the man I will wed? As though *I* am not the one who must *live* with him! My entire life!"

Her father's low voice remained as inflexible as ever. "When you have learned the danger of hasty words, then—and only then

—will I share what few know. Until that day, content yourself with the fact that you are not espoused to any man."

What few know? Nay, she would not be distracted. She forced her words past set teeth. "I will not wed Ivan Maerton!"

He captured her hands. "Daughter! Cease these declarations. In moments, we will walk down the stairs and join your peers. Is this the mien you intend to show them?"

She realized her posture, the tension in her face. Did she look enraged? Once again, she had behaved as a child—or so her mother would say. Straightening, she calmed her voice. "Nay, I will show only the respect you are due. But, Father, how am I to convey the depth of my concern in this matter?"

"As though I am in doubt!" He tapped a finger against her chin. "Do I not care for you, m'Beth? Have I not said that you are *not* espoused?"

She melted as he used the endearing name of old. "Forgive me, Father." Her tone was perfect, and his face yielded. She opened and closed her mouth, longing to ask what he'd meant a moment ago.

"Speak, my child."

"When you tell me…'what few know'…will you also show me the rest of Lavaycia?"

The creases deepened in his brow. "What fancy is this? You have seen Lavaycia."

"The duchies, aye, but not the lands north. The Tower Woods and beyond to the River Thane."

His blond eyebrows jutted. He seemed to find it hard to speak. "You have no idea what you ask!"

Never had she seen such a strange expression pass over his face.

CHAPTER 9

The Castle in the Wilde

Tristan joined James and Cotrell in a vain search through the cellars. Instead of tunnels or a hidden entrance, they found provisions and wine bottles with unreadable labels. James shook his head. "Whatever they used for ink, was not up to their typical standards."

Tristan and Cotrell left James when he discovered the kitchen well, a covered bin of firewood, and a washtub.

"How can he think about washing clothes?" Cotrell murmured in the bailey.

"I don't know, but I admit, I'll don fresh linens with pleasure." Tristan headed first for the stable. "Let's get our bows in case we spot something for dinner."

They gave each tower a careful inspection. All differed, for bedrock dictated their foundations.

They ended at the square northwest tower and climbed first to its height. Cantilevers supported a western extension, which provided a view down the cliff face. A waterfall gushed from its base, creating a valley stream. Tristan studied the bare rock. No beast could climb that. On the orchard side, he could just make out a ledge before the cliff plummeted. "Let's go down," he said.

Cotrell grunted, his gaze on a flock of ducks passing over.

At the foundation level, Tristan stared. This was wrong. He looked up to see Cotrell's reaction as he descended.

He paused halfway down the steps. "Where's the rest of it?"

"Indeed!" Tristan inspected the stone wall that cut off half the tower room. "'Tis solid." He strode out the door and skirted the structure that abutted the tower. He turned the corner by the wall and stopped short. "We were looking for tunnels..." He uttered a disbelieving laugh. "And there is a gate!"

Cotrell halted next to him. "But to where? There was but a single gate on the orchard side, and that is back along the north wall."

"Only one way to find out."

Tristan led the way down the slope to a swing gate wide enough for one horse. An archway beside them supported the tower wall and gave access to the lower half of the foundation room. They peered inside.

"Could be a guard room." Tristan pointed to iron bars beside the gate. "It can be barred from this side—but 'tis not."

He lifted an iron latch—which scraped far more than he expected—and pulled. The gate swung inward on a pivot. 'Twas surprisingly thick, for the outside bore a layer of stone.

"Would that I could meet the architect! I wager there is a cleverly hidden latch outside."

Cotrell shook his head. "I'll not wager against that certainty."

Tristan studied the gate and its frame. "Three latches..." he murmured, then stepped beyond. "Open it in five minutes if I don't get through." The gate swung shut under its own weight. It took him a few minutes, but he knew what he was looking for and soon pushed the gate open. He grinned at Cotrell. "Come out. There are three hidden levers which must be worked in the correct sequence. I'll show you. Then we can see where this path leads."

Cotrell mastered the mechanism, and with a satisfied nod, let the gate shut again. "Clever, but I no longer believe that only Burk's father knew the hidden way."

"Nay, for that was a child's understanding. No one else in their town knew. This is hidden from outsiders, not the castle residents." Tristan turned. "And now, for this path."

"Which I will walk ahead of you."

Tristan raised his brows at Cotrell.

"As I should have done with that tree." Cotrell maneuvered past him. "A century of rain can pierce solid rock, and if you did not want my protection, you should not have given me the rank of captain." Cotrell strode ahead of him without waiting for an answer.

Just as well. Prudence bade Tristan hold his tongue, and he was not fond of prudence. Still, Cotrell had a valid point. Tristan followed him along the path, which was, in fact, the ledge he'd seen from above. Bare rock on the right, a precipice on the left. He could imagine some horses—even some men—balking at the sight of it. They walked below the tangled hedge of the orchard. The ledge descended, though gradually. Farther on, it widened and merged with a valley in the woodland beyond the orchard.

He and Cotrell surveyed it in silence, bows in hand. They couldn't even see the castle from here. A flock of elderbirds meandered between trees, pecking at the ground.

Tristan barely heard Cotrell whisper, "You take the nearest... on three." They raised their bows. "One, two, three."

Both arrows found their marks, Cotrell's an instant kill. Tristan's wounded the bird, and it flailed, squawking, as the rest of the flock flapped awkwardly into low flight.

Cotrell ran forward and dispatched the injured bird.

Tristan nocked another arrow and watched the woods until Cotrell returned with both birds...and a grin. "Let's get back. If he cannot find us, even James might get frantic."

They ate in the kitchen and—clean at last—slept in fine beds. Plans formulated in Tristan's mind, even within dreams, it seemed.

WHEN THEY'D BROKEN their fast, Tristan said, "Let's go up to the roof. I noticed a fair amount of green from above and would know what it is."

They used the north tower, where the fifth-level door opened to the roof. Tristan paused and stared up the winding steps. "What's up there, Cotrell?"

"'Tis the domain of an artistic lady. Dainty furniture, unfinished paintings, and drawings with intricate detail. 'Twould not surprise me, were I told that she drew the map I studied."

Tristan nodded and followed James across the roof. The green shapes he'd seen from above were raised, weedy beds, some with slatted cedar coverings.

"I believe the family lounged up here," James said, pointing at bare frames as they followed the parapet. "Awnings could have hung from these. I noticed simple chairs and tables in the fourth-floor storage, which I now suspect may be intended for the roof."

Cotrell paused to look down on the bailey, but Tristan continued around with James.

"You may have noticed, my lord, that the roof slopes gently westward." James pointed out structures near that wall. "The excess rainwater drains on the ends." He looked over the parapet. "They may have collected it too."

The two men angled back toward the north tower and stopped by a bed that curved around its base. Some unique plants battled the weeds for space.

Cotrell sauntered over, as James said, "'Tis an herb garden. Here is thyme, which grows anywhere, but look, my lord— *rosemary*."

What was so special about that?

Cotrell quirked an eyebrow. "So...our meat will be tastier tonight?"

James closed his eyes, before turning back to Tristan. "Rosemary cannot survive the winters in Moorelin. The local climate must be more temperate, the winters mild."

"Ah," Tristan murmured, "and here I thought you were commending the self-sufficiency this castle provides."

"Aye, that too. More so than any of Moorelin."

Tristan looked to the woods. "It had to. I've seen no sign that dwellings stood beyond the walls. Strange to see a castle without a village."

"Perhaps there was not time for a village to form," James said. "Though this castle has stood empty for decades, I do not think it is very old."

"Nay, the stone has not deteriorated." Tristan strolled toward a marble statue of a woman and child, surrounded by benches. He sat on one of them. "What would it take to occupy this castle?"

"I wondered when you'd get around to that question," Cotrell said.

"'Twas inevitable." James sat on a bench angled toward Tristan. "Before occupying, you should consider whether you can *hold* the castle. Perhaps it has no village because of the beasts. All of them."

Cotrell braced a foot against a bench and crossed his arms on his knee. "With enough men, we can deal with wolves and bears, even big ones. Vixicats are another matter." He looked to Tristan. "Have you read more of that journal?"

"Some. If the cycle documented by the last master is real, we will need our own observations to see where we lie within it." Tristan considered for a moment. "He never studied them over winter. I'm not even sure how late in autumn they stayed or how early in spring they returned."

"I may be able to determine that from the ledgers," James said.

Tristan nodded. "Please do so. To truly determine whether I can hold the castle and surrounding land, I must make the attempt. But the hazards are not to be taken lightly. I cannot ask men to bring their families here. They must be able to come ahead and prepare for families to join them later. Not too many men, but enough to clear the near woods, repair the damage of neglect, and meet the needs of daily life." He tilted his head. "And to defend the castle, should the need arise."

"The archers who followed you into battle," Cotrell said. "Most are young. Many had already begun learning professions of one sort or another, which could prove useful. Best of all, we know their determination against a ruthless enemy. We could gather them and return in spring."

"I would rather bring families in spring or summer, thus I'd prefer to gather men at once and winter here."

Cotrell's brows shot up. "Have we time?"

"That, we will determine today," Tristan said. "And more, as well. How many men do we need? What skills are critical? What provisions must be brought? We must also assess what the castle holds, and what more we require for this venture to work. Tomorrow morn we leave."

The men were silent until James said, "I will perform a general inventory, but realize, it will be imprecise."

Tristan nodded. "That will be adequate."

Cotrell frowned in thought. "What you need most would lie outside the castle, not within it." He lowered his foot from the bench. "A road and a bridge, my lord."

"Ah! You are right." He met Cotrell's gaze for a moment. "How could we accomplish that on the way here?"

"Before we reach the castle?" James asked.

"Aye. If we must camp, I would rather do it on the north side of the ridge. From the journal, 'tis clear that the vixicats have a set range. If they ever crossed the ridge, we would have heard stories from the travelers to Fountain Isle. That side is safer until we can get the bridge rebuilt. Then, we could bring provisions to the castle within a day. Wagons, maybe livestock, with mounted archers to guard them."

Cotrell rubbed his chestnut beard and answered slowly. "Could be done."

Tristan stood. "Then, we must consider how long it will take, and whether we should fell local timber or bring it all the way from Moorelin. Captain D'Jorge can decide that and obtain the tools and supplies. You and Captain Wellinstine can help me choose and assemble the men."

BEFORE TWILIGHT, Tristan went up to his bedroom and felt within the inner pouch of his saddle pack. His finger touched cool metal, and he pulled out his signet ring. He'd not worn it since he left the elegant cities of Verenlia. But now, he had a decision to make. Though nothing need be written, still it seemed that the ring should witness their discussion over dinner and his final choice.

He slipped it on and headed back toward the central stairs. The carved wooden doors of the chapel caught his eye. He'd had no time to see it at sunset. 'Twould only take a moment. He crossed the corridor and opened the double doors.

The effect was all he'd hoped and more. The prisms scattered brilliant colors, but the stained-glass radiated a light of its own, bathing the white marble table with a second rainbow. Yet the thing he noticed most was…a feeling beyond words. As though the light had taken on a living presence.

He approached the table, the carpet hushing his footsteps, and rested his hand within the rainbow. The symbol of hope and protection. Hope. The castle already sparked it within him. Protection. He—all of them—would need that if they were to hold this land. He dropped to one knee and wordlessly asked for the light of wisdom. The advice of James and Cotrell, he must yet give ear to, but one thing was certain. Forever would he yearn for this place if he did not return.

AFTER DINNER, they rested in the library amid dusty books and a fine collection of marble carvings. James had gone off somewhere, but his inventories lay on the desk with the map under Tristan's hand. Their discussion at dinner of *whether* to return had soon shifted into plans for how *best* to return.

The fullness in his chest...He hadn't felt this since...ah, since his father had given him his signet ring. The soft glow of candlelight flickered over the carved gold as it had that night in his father's library.

Cotrell must have noticed where his gaze rested, for he said, "'Tis fitting that you wear your ring again, my lord."

Tristan let out a long breath. "Aye."

The door opened, and James entered, a tray in hand.

Tristan's smile slowly formed. "What have you there?"

James placed it on a sideboard. "'Tis unnamed like all the rest, my lord, but I think you will find it palatable." He lifted the cloth draped over the bottle and began pouring into three wine glasses.

"What is this?" Cotrell said. "Have you tasted it without us?"

"Be glad that I did." James angled a look toward him. "The first one I opened was vile beyond description. This came from another rack." He offered the first goblet to Tristan, who had come to stand before the empty fireplace. James and Cotrell took the other two.

Tristan inhaled the aroma, then took a sip. Mellow with the hint of a foreign fruit. "Mm. This is remarkably good!"

"Aye," Cotrell murmured.

"I thought it would be suitable for a first toast, my lord."

"Ah, James, you are right, as always." Tristan raised his glass. "To the Castle in the Wilde."

Glass chinked as they responded, and Cotrell said, "The Castle in the Wilde—with an *e*."

Tristan chuckled and gestured to the heavy leather chairs around the hearth. "Sit, my friends." He settled, resting one hand on the armrest as he enjoyed another sip.

Again, the signet ring drew his eye. Candlelight danced over the outline of his family's crest, which circled the prominent *P*. Symbols shared by all five Petram brothers. Memory stirred— the first time he'd seen his initial *T* entwined through the Petram crest. This ring...somehow his father felt near, as in the days when they searched for Tristan's future estate.

James broke his abstraction. "Have you thought much of what your brother might say?"

His *eldest* brother, of course. Tristan answered only to him. "Not greatly, but I do not think he will forbid. I'll send a letter to him by express courier after we cross the River Thane into Moorelin."

They enjoyed their wine in silence for a few minutes. Tristan glanced from one to the other and drew a deep breath. "I have led you now into something you never agreed to when we set out from Moorelin. An endeavor that could cost lives. Know that you are free to choose whether you return with me."

Cotrell tilted his head back to laugh. "Do not think that I'll let you take this venture without me."

James smiled, sedate as always. "I would rather steward your estate than your travels."

Warmth spread through Tristan's chest. He'd expected such answers, but they were nonetheless pleasing, for that.

CHAPTER 10

Castle in the Wilde

Tristan locked the hidden gate. Deep shadow cloaked it, for the rising sun still filtered through trees on the eastern hills. He followed the ledge to the valley, where Cotrell and James met him with the horses, and there he mounted Dauntless. "Cotrell, you lead. James, follow him. I'll take the rear."

They found the northeast road. Parts of it were still clear, and they made good time to the ridge, cresting it at noon. Tristan paused astride Dauntless, gazing down on the wooded hills. Familiar enough now that he could even find the tower peaks among the leafless branches. Like a new acquaintance. Known—but slightly.

What of Lavaycia? So near, yet intentionally absent. Where did their actual border lie? The mystery of the castle's original owners still troubled him. Might Lavaycians know more? If so, how might that affect his plans? Certain he was, that the former owners had not been killed by vixicats. But why did they never return?

What if their descendants still remembered? What if they returned at some future time? By Moorelin's law, property abandoned for fifty years was free to anyone who could hold it. But this was not Moorelin. 'Twas not any country, for not a soul lived in The Wilde.

Why did he ponder anything so unlikely? He would find no answer by staring at hills! He guided Dauntless over to join Cotrell and James atop the north descent.

Cotrell shaded his eyes with a hand, gazing northwest. "Fountain Isle still looks quiet."

"Hm." Tristan frowned.

"We could ride there first, if you are concerned," James suggested.

Ah, those hot spring pools would feel good! His lingering aches begged for that relief. Tempting. "Nay," he said. "I've no true cause for worry. We must hasten. We've much to do, and the time is short. Let us descend."

Why did that sensible decision feel so wrong?

SHARE THE ADVENTURE

I hope you found something in these pages that made your life a little richer. If you liked this story, maybe others would too. You can help them find it by leaving a brief review or even by clicking some stars wherever you like to purchase or review books. Those star ratings and reviews help me, too, and I greatly appreciate all of them.

Would you like to read more stories like this one? If so, I invite you to join my newsletter. I will send you some free short stories, share a little about life, and let you know about new books and an occasional sale. I won't overload your inbox or share your email address with others. You may unsubscribe at any time. Sign up at SharonRoseAuthor.com. I hope to hear from you!

THE NEXT ADVENTURE

A Castle Awakened

Castle in the Wilde: Novel 1

A foreign usurper. A lady who longs for freedom. Secrets more dangerous than beasts.

Never one to shy from a challenge, Lord Petram took possession of a forsaken castle. His search uncovered no hint of who built it or why they abandoned such a gem. What treachery would strike the founding family from history? Still, it seems a small matter, since the generations have passed. If he and his followers can forge a life here—and hold out against ravenous vixicats—the castle and this land will be theirs. As for the nearest kingdom, they never venture beyond their border or the mysterious forest of tower trees. Except...

Beth dons a disguise and takes a forbidden ride in Tower Woods—a last fling before she bows to the dictates of her noble birth. Her fun adventure turns into a nightmare of kidnap and rescue—of sorts. Now she's trapped in a nameless castle held by a foreign usurper who calls himself Lord Petram. Who could he be, and what will he do with her if he finds out who she really is?

Thus, Lord Petram finds himself the unwilling guardian of an injured lady who won't give her full name. A crime he didn't commit may bring retribution from an unknown kingdom. Do they have a claim to this castle that he now calls home? If he survives the vixicats, will an army slaughter him and his followers?

A Castle Awakened is the first novel in the *Castle in the Wilde* trilogy. If you like fantasy with mystery, intrigue, and romance, come and explore this secondary world with medieval undertones and the turmoil of clashing cultures.

Interested? Ask your favorite bookstore or library for:

A Castle Awakened, by Sharon Rose, ISBN: 978-1-948160-21-6

ACKNOWLEDGMENTS

Thankfulness is one of those intangible acts that costs nothing but gives joy. Think about it. Not only does it bring a smile to the people who receive our thanks. It also increases our own appreciation of everything we receive. A sunset, a flower, a song, an encouraging word, a kind deed, a gift, even a payment we are due. Receiving them thankfully adds a polishing touch to the treasure.

This world we live in dishes out plenty to drag us down, so letting joy flourish is all the more crucial. Join me in thinking of treasures to be thankful for.

I'll start because, yeah, this is the acknowledgements, after all!

Family support is foundational to my writing. Husband, children, siblings, in-laws, even grandkids now. My thanks to all of you for everything from encouragement to taking care of the practical things of life.

Bridgett Powers, my faithful editor and friend. Thanks for always being there for me. You know my books wouldn't be published without you.

Kirk DouPonce, thank you for your always-fabulous cover design and for art that reflects what I have written.

Matthew Ferguson, thank you for the medieval style maps to give substance to my fantasy world, and especially, for the vixicat in the corner.

Realm Makers—the conference, the online community, the people: This tribe, who understands both faith and speculative fiction, has made a huge difference in my author journey. Many thanks to all of you.

Write Now writer's group at Living Word Christian Center: You are delightful friends and encouragers. Thank you for listening to me read and giving me feedback.

Advance Readers: Though I will never see most of you face-to-face, the time you take to read, review, and spread the word, means more than you realize. Those of you who have sent me personal notes, your kind words are priceless.

To *all* of my readers: Even though these words are printed before you read this book, I feel as much gratitude for you as for everyone mentioned above. You've taken the time to walk a story-journey with me, and I don't take that for granted. I hope you've found something in it to bring light and joy to your days.

Now it's your turn. What are you thankful for, right in this moment?

ABOUT THE AUTHOR

I started writing when I was seven years old. Okay, *My Life as a Flying Squirrel* may have had a couple spelling errors, but my classmates loved it.

Plenty of life has happened since that first story, and I've come to realize the things that fascinate me. People. Communication. Culture. Personality. Viewpoints. Beliefs. Anything that makes each of us beautifully unique. Small wonder that my art spills out in story form.

It was only a matter of time, before I just had to share my stories. I've published science fiction and now fantasy, two genres that allow us to explore reality while having fun.

When I'm not writing or reading, I may be traveling, enjoying gardens, or searching for unique coffee shops with my husband. We live in Minnesota, USA, famed for its mosquitoes —uh, I mean 10,000 lakes and vibrant seasons.

To find out more, visit SharonRoseAuthor.com.

Follow me on:
Amazon, Goodreads, BookBub, and Facebook.
Find all of my links at: https://linktr.ee/sharonrose.author